THE MYSTERIOUS LETTER:
Aunt Lee's Legacy

By Marie Therese

Copyright © 2013 Marie Therese
All rights reserved
First Edition

PAGE PUBLISHING, INC.
New York, NY

First originally published by Page Publishing 2013

ISBN 978-1-62838-090-3 (pbk)
ISBN 978-1-62838-091-0 (digital)

Printed in the United States of America

Dear Jayla,
I hope you enjoy reading my book as much as I did writing it.
Love,
Marie Therese

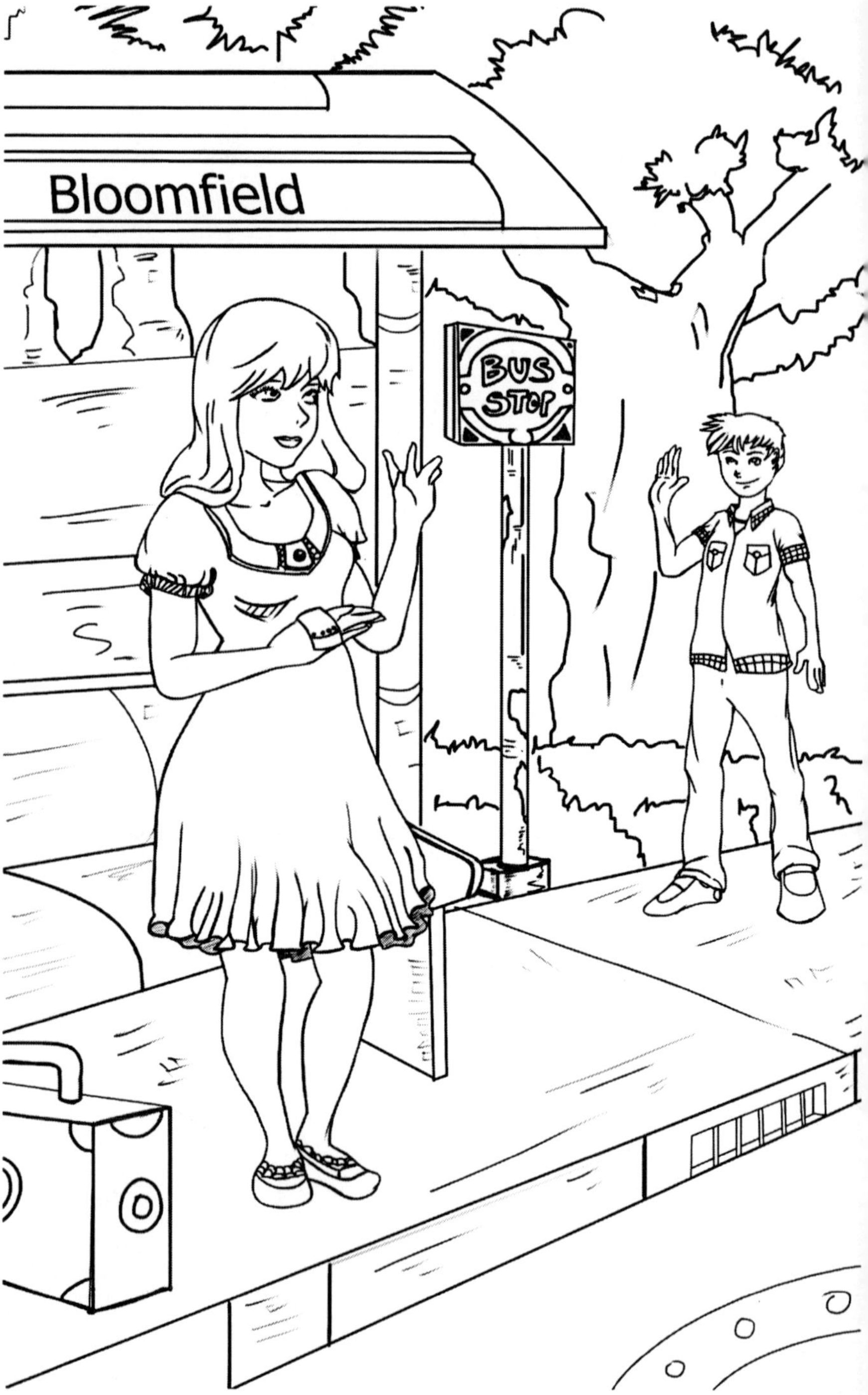
Bloomfield
BUS STOP

Chapter 1
The Mysterious Letter

The penmanship in the letter was shaky and its content could be boiled down to just one frantic word: "COME!"

My name is Cassie. It was 6:15 in the morning, and I was standing at the bus terminal.

The letter from Aunt Lee had arrived the day before, calling for immediate action.

Josh, my brother, read the letter and was also convinced that our aunt was in distress. He admitted that my trip was a good idea and I promised to call him daily with news. I was a little nervous about the trip.

Well, not the trip really, but what was going on with Aunt Lee to make her summon me in such a hasty way? I knew I was mature enough to meet this problem head on.

Aunt Lee is an exciting character. She is my hero, and traveled around the world and wrote about her experiences for a popular magazine. I followed her escapades by reading my own personal copy of the periodical. A collection of artifacts and souvenirs of the trips jogged her memory about each destination.

Aunt Lee sent a letter every spring to Mom asking for me to come and visit for two weeks in the summer. I looked forward to these visits with the anticipation of much fun.

MARIE THERESE

Two years ago this all changed when Mom and Dad died in an automobile accident. Aunt Lee arrived late at the funeral after canceling a trip to New Guinea, and exhibited emotions of great sorrow for her sister's death.

Tears and sobs wracked her petite frame with waves of uncontrolled grief.

The following Fall, Josh entered college and I went to a small boarding school that boasted year-round living quarters. The dorm rooms were large and my roommate was a little ball of fun from Tennessee. Her antics usually kept my spirits from dipping too low when the sad memories set in.

I do not get mail often, only from Josh. When Aunt Lee's letter arrived, I hoped it would bring an upturn to my boring life.

I re-read the letter on the bus. This was not the same letter I usually received from Aunt Lee. Written on lavender-scented paper, I noticed suspicious water stains here and there. I read the pages over and over in hopes of finding out what the problem was.

Was Aunt Lee in trouble? Had she been sick or hurt? Had she, on one of her many tropical travels, had a spell put on her or tasted some potion that had affected her mind? My imagination raced. Finally, exhausted from worry I fell asleep, and woke up in New York City.

Out the window of the bus I spotted Matthew, Aunt Lee's trusted houseman. I stepped down from the bus and followed him to Aunt Lee's black Mercedes. Twenty minutes of honking horns, flashing lights, and screaming sirens later, we entered a quiet area of elegant brownstones, one of which was Aunt Lee's.

I followed Matthew through the huge carved front door and up the steps to the second floor bedroom where I spent prior summer visits. Everything was just as I had left it. Warm feelings mixed with a strange emptiness fluttered through my body. Alone again, I unpacked the old battered suitcase I inherited from Dad.

Soon Matthew knocked on my door and stated, "Miss Lee requests your presence in her sitting room." The sitting room was a combination office/ library/ clutter-bin, in which she worked and relaxed. I loved that room, it was charged with unseen energy and full of life with its various contents, I never got bored just sitting and looking around. Aunt Lee usually buzzed around the room, talking on the telephone, dictating memos, or listening to animal sounds from CDs.

I was unprepared for what happened next.

I walked into the sitting room and there on the leather lounge chair Aunt Lee reclined, wrapped up in a comforter, looking like one of the china dolls she had sent me from an Asia trip. Matthew served lemon tea bread and Earl Grey tea, a ritual we always observed.

Quickly getting over my shock, I realized what was happening to Aunt Lee: she was getting older and had decided to fade gracefully into the twilight of her life.

A short time later, I understood the answer to the summons. Aunt Lee wanted to pass on an account of life-long adventures, her legacy, to me. She was sure that during the process we could help each other deal with the loneliness hidden within each of us.

Aunt Lee and I decided to live together in the big townhouse while I enrolled in a school specializing in foreign cultural studies. I helped Aunt Lee reminisce, and then record the wonderful events she experienced throughout her life. Her spirits have improved and my outlook on life is much more hopeful now.

It's funny how one mysterious letter can change two lives so much.

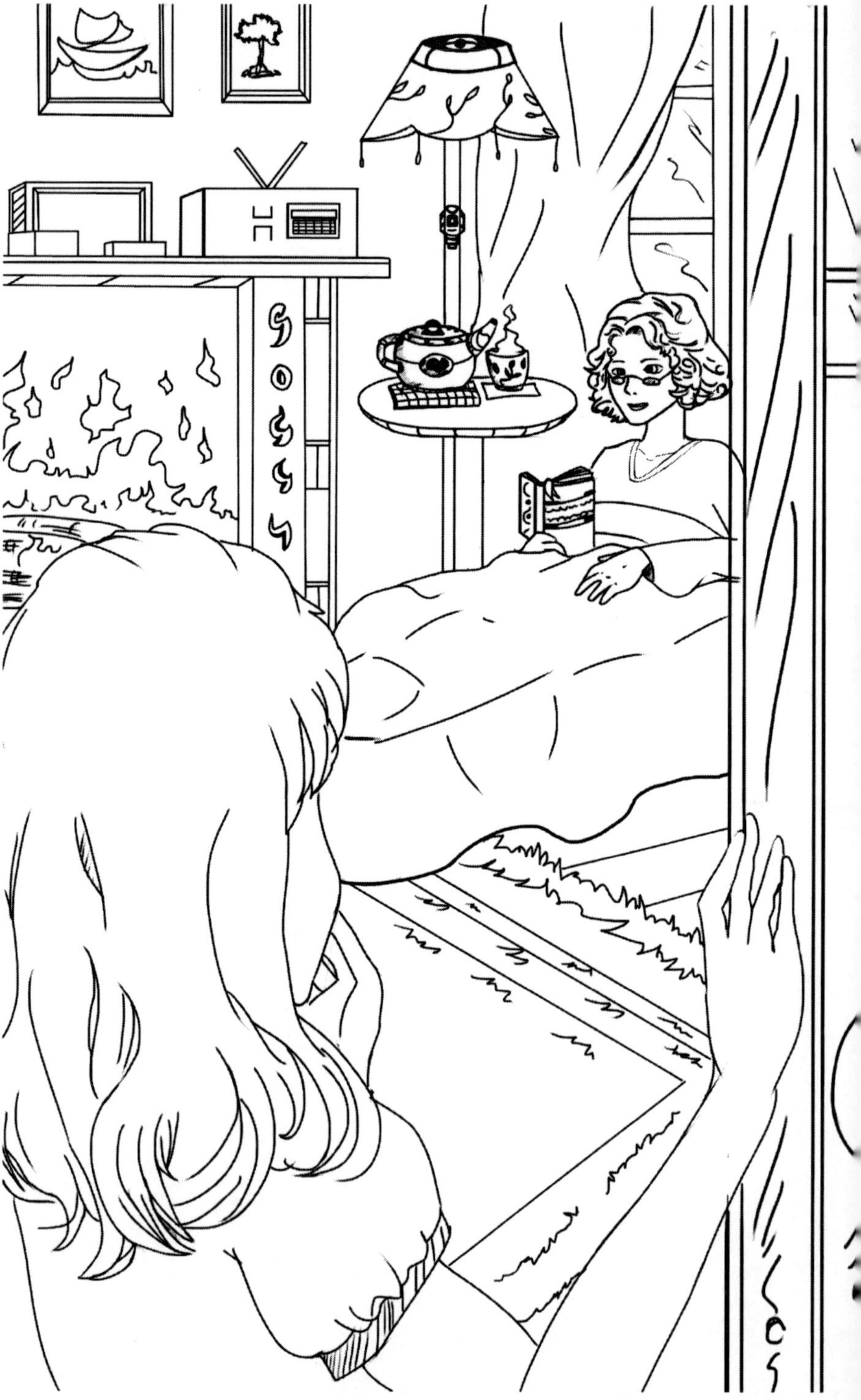

Chapter 2
The Ritual

Aunt Lee and I had a daily ritual, this combined afternoon tea and discussions about which exotic travel destination we would write.

Matthew would arrive in the den at exactly 3:30 p.m., carrying an ornate silver tea service with Earl Grey tea and the ever-delicious lemon tea bread. The delicate yellow tea bread, lightly brushed with powdered sugar, smelled like a freshly sliced lemon, both sweet and tangy.

Each evening after schoolwork, I would study travel, geography and vacation books about the country we were to work on the following afternoon. I would try to commit to memory facts like capital cities, imports and exports, native customs and religious beliefs.

My aunt often needed a nudge from me to overcome the memory lapses that plagued her recitations. Sometimes while speaking on a subject, Aunt Lee would suddenly become silent and stare off at the charming watercolored silk wall coverings. I had trouble deciding if she was just re-living a wonderful memory, or had at that moment lost her thoughts entirely. Most times I would hesitate a bit, then mention the previous few sentences I had recorded. This tactic usually gently sparked a fuse in her brain and she would amble on, totally enveloping me in the story. Luckily, the times she actually nodded off were few. These times saddened me, for I didn't want to lose my aunt now, after feeling as though I had just found her. I always ignored the little lapses of time, and felt that she too appreciated my discretion.

I could fully appreciate the reason why so many travel magazines always pursued the adventures of my aunt. She had a special talent for not only sharing the wonders of her experiences, but also making a reader feel as if they were joining right in with the activities. A reader could close their eyes and envision the land, the people, and the atmosphere of any exotic location about which she was writing. My chore was to capture the essence of her adventures and convey them through written words.

Little did I realize what a challenge and an exciting venture this would become for me. Through Aunt Lee's words I began to re-live her unconventional and sometimes daring lifestyle. The very first afternoon we spent working together, I learned some shocking and unexpected facts about my genteel aunt which had here-to fore remained secret.

Chapter 3
Egypt

A personality trait of choice belonging to Lee was that of observant silence. Many years of experience taught her that to really see and ultimately record the culture of a country, one must surreptitiously observe its people in respectful quiet. Little did she know, this very same trait would cause some local inhabitants of the exotic country of Egypt to quake and shake in their sandals.

A leisurely boat ride on the gentle waters of the Nile inspired thoughts of long ago when Egyptian Pharaohs used their wealth for extreme pleasure and self satisfaction. The river rippled and swayed against the brightly colored transport vessel, and Lee allowed her imagination to take her back in time to when the Valley of the Kings was in its glorious realm of construction. Closed eyes allowed vivid visions of grandeur and gold. Palm fronds cooled the watchful eyes of the rich as they beheld their future homes of death. Baskets of dried fruits and nuts were amassed as food for the protective gods. Words and pictures were colorfully etched in the stone walls, depicting the life-actions of citizens. Amulets, artifacts and jewels declared the extent of a family's wealth. Secret passageways and hidden doors held secrets not to be revealed.

Though Lee was engrossed in daydreams, loud mumbling invaded her peaceful mind-massage. She woke to find several of the local people surrounding her and staring, pointing to her face. Wondering what the problem was, Lee reached into her travel satchel and retrieved a small makeup mirror. When she removed her polarized sunglasses to peer into the imaging tool, several gasps caused her to look up rapidly.

Behind the sheltering lenses, Lee's eyes were the color blue that could only be compared to lapis lazuli, a precious stone found in this ancient countryside. Besides the startling color, the size of her eyes and the long jet eyelashes often caused stares and comments from admirers. Lee was comfortable with ordinary appreciation of her physical appearance, but this time the attention was unsettling. Gasps grew into moans and even shouts, while elderly boat travelers fell to their knees and covered their heads.

Seeing the commotion, an astute steward politely pushed his way through the throng of people and gently led Lee to a private stateroom frequented by the crew. The steward kindly offered an explanation to the cause of the commotion.

He explained that the land of Egypt is heavily steeped in mythology and religious superstition, gods rule every aspect of both daily life and death. These gods sometimes have likenesses that can be adored and prayed to. Icons, pictures, and statues depict the physical portrayals of the gods.

The goddess of the mountain overlooking the Valley of the Kings is known as Meretseger, or "she who loves silence". A cobra goddess, Meretseger would spit venom at anyone who attempted to disturb the tombs. Revered by the inhabitants of Deir ei-Medina (the people who were responsible for building the tombs), she struck out at workers who committed crimes. Besides being silent and watchful, Meretseger was said to possess the most astonishing bright blue eyes. Workers could not look into her eyes for fear that she would see their bad thoughts or evil doings.

In her presence they would bend in supplication and cover their heads.

The travelers on the slow moving barge had ample time to allow their imaginations to soar. Aunt Lee was an unusually silent person who seemed to be drinking in the local atmosphere as though her mind was parched and searching for libation. Then, to confirm the travelers' fears, her astounding blue eyes caught each one of the rowdy offenders. Idle minds, along with guilty consciences, fueled the superstitious followers to brand Lee as a goddess, sent there to make them accountable for their crimes.

The steward, an educated young man, apologized to Lee and offered her a honeyed drink, laced with lemon and ice. She accepted gladly and thanked him for his astute observation of a strange situation.

At Thebes, Lee disembarked from the sloop and made sure her sunglasses were securely over her eyes. She headed directly for the nearest library, where she spent a few hours investigating her own private goddess, Meretseger. Though the established cult of faithful followers of Meretseger had mysteriously died out in the XXI dynasty, the faithful still paid her homage.

The following day the tour of the Valley of the Kings was even more impressive now that Lee knew there was a special goddess who watched over the tombs and had eyes the exact color of hers.

Chapter 4
Haiti

We chose our writing subjects by global regions. Actually, we closed our eyes, spun the world globe, and wherever the globe stopped would be our next choice. Our very first spin caused Aunt Lee to describe a tense adventure that happened in Haiti, an interesting country in the Caribbean Ocean.

Seasoned journalists know that tourist traps are the last places to really learn about the genuine habitats of native peoples. Therefore, unconventional methods are used to extract information from local dwellers. Bribes, gifts, dinners and casual flirting are all acceptable precoursers for the validation of little known facts. Aunt Lee was well aware of these tactics and regularly made use of them to gain food for her cookbook of gourmet journalistic treasures.

I researched the small, but historically rich, country of Haiti. Familiar with her method of research, I knew that Aunt Lee would have delved deep into the religious background of the country, and searched relentlessly for juicy tidbits about its famous practice of voodoo. My fascination with the forceful passion of this religion kept me reading late into the night. I had difficulty falling asleep in anticipation of our time tomorrow when I would hear an undoubtedly vivid replay of Aunt Lee's interaction with an ancient, and possibly malevolent cult.

HAITI

Aunt Lee was known by her fellow travel buffs for her petite stature, natural beauty, and exuberant mannerisms. These qualities were quite often a detriment to her ability to keep timely schedules. She embraced life and all of its people and things with positive passion. Although these might be perceived as good qualities to have, it also brought about expressions of jealousy from those who possessed less of a flavor for life. Lee's refreshing display of innocence was almost her downfall amongst the exotic palms and vibrant tropical birds in Haiti.

My research told me that the Voodoo religion, a product of slave trade, was brought to Haiti by the African slaves. It migrated with the slaves to other communities such as New Orleans, Miami and New York City, fifty million followers made up these communities.

Rituals involving drums, dancing and chants were performed to serve or request help or good fortune from the gods, or Loa. A community of practitioners, or société, was made up of organized and devoted followers.

Lee interviewed active members of the société along with a few priests and priestesses. She spent days living among the devotees and actually
participated in some of the musical, colorful rituals. Her instincts carried feelings of goodness for these ardent, happy people.

However, as every light side has a dark side, so did this honored religion also have a reverse conscience. The product of this was known as "Black Magic." Black Magic seemed to be a resting-place for all the malevolent dropouts of the voodoo community. Malcontents needed an organized way to invoke harm on others that had gained fortune or disagreed with their doctrines. They used horrific human sacrifices and cannibalism, and conjured up the dead to perform evil acts on enemies.

Lee's curiosity was piqued as she walked among the street vendors in Port au-Prince. Common knowledge told her that these outdoor shopkeepers knew more confidential information than any of the local newspapers or tourist guidebooks. Innocent inquiry opened up channels of discreet conversations and directions to the Black Magic havens.

An old crone, sitting in between two booths selling talismans and love potions, beckoned Aunt Lee to come to her side. Lee answered the summons and was rewarded by a cautious whispering voice telling her of a secret ceremony to be held that very night. Superstitious warnings went unheeded and Lee, delighted by her discovery, traced her steps back to her hotel to rest.

After studying the sketchy directions and comparing them to a street map, Lee ventured out to find the hidden sepulchre of forbidden rights. Miles later, damp, clammy breezes drifted around ancient mausoleums within an old French cemetery which smelled of decay and mold. Luckily it was still daylight so she could carefully trudge through the overgrown vines and dead foliage without injury. The cemetery was ancient and very large. Mausoleums and whole-family plots took up a vast amount of the walled-in home of the dead.

In the exact middle of the property there was an area strictly devoted to the burial of slaves who had belonged to the French settlers. Though most were marked with small, unembellished headstones, some actually had little houses which were exact replicas of the large manor homes of years gone by. Lee had read that some slaves became so endeared to the families that they were honored in death with almost as much respect as the landowners.

It was by one of these crypts that the Black Magic display was performed. Muted drums beaten in eerie cadence lured Lee into the melee. Red and white clad bodies writhed and swayed to a hypnotic rhythm. The chants were loud and repetitive and the participants jostled and bumped each other constantly.

Perspiring profusely, Lee bobbed in and among the devoted, and headed towards a table which held earthenware pitchers of a cool looking red liquid. The heat and humidity had drained her body of moisture, and her common sense was replaced with an intense thirst. A cool glass of iced punch was just what Lee had in mind to quench her parched throat.

She grabbed one of the crude, heavy pitchers and poured herself a full glass of libation. Just as she was about to drink, a woman dressed in ceremonial garb grabbed her wrist. Gold bracelets jangled and vibrant colors swirled as the woman shook her head rapidly and shouted, "No drink!"

Startled, Lee put down the glass and cowered defensively. The woman, obviously a priestess, continued to hold her wrist and pulled her over to a shaded overhang of the stone burial home. Managing to control her fright, Lee considered that subservience would be the best choice for her at this time.

Once away from the chaos, the admitted priestess offered an explanation for her actions.

Lee was totally unaware of the consequences that could have occurred if she had drank the red liquid in the pitcher. It contained an important part of the ceremonial ritual, the base of the unctuous concoction was made up of pureed dead animal parts. Various herbs had been added to invoke the pleasures of the gods and hopefully inspire them to grant favors. Ice was added to keep it from becoming rancid and draw insects or other parasites to the mixture. Worst of all was the addition of curare, a poisonous ingredient that could at least paralyze, and at most, kill humans. Lee thanked the priestess and realized her good fortune.

The priestess would not admit the exact purpose of the potion, but Lee surmised that it was used in regular rituals by the followers of the religious sect.

Although the priestess was kind, she was also elusive about what was to happen next.

Resting from the ordeal, Lee watched intently when a scantily garbed male member of the group danced over to the table with the pitchers and promptly guzzled down a full glass of the elixir. He then began whirling like a dervish, alternating chants with shouts. His body gleaming with sweat, as he finally collapsed in the center of the circle. A black shroud of silky material was placed over his body. Forced composure allowed Lee to stay put and wait for the outcome.

Each member of the group slowly tiptoed up to the black shrouded man and placed a shiny stone on the edge of the blanket. After everyone had contributed, they held hands in a tight circle and swayed to an unheard melody. Chanting began slowly and increased in volume until the din was deafening. Suddenly, a scream erupted from the center of the circle. The black sheet floated upward, and the prone man gracefully rose to his feet. His hands were folded in prayer and his eyes lifted upwards. The sheet floated to the ground and the man slowly walked through the open wooden door of the mausoleum. The heavy door closed behind him.

Lee, totally immersed in the actions of the man, turned quickly around. She was utterly shocked to find that she was the only person there! The exit of the group, including the priestess, had been silent and swift. Lee turned back to the lichen- encrusted building and stepped gingerly to the old wooden door. Increased emotions quickened her heartbeat when she saw that the door was not only padlocked with a huge rusty lock; but moss and other parasitic plant life were twisted and gnarled between the door and the stones of the building.

Instant observation yielded that NO ONE could have opened this door for many, many years.

Realizing that panic was futile, Lee confusingly backtracked through the cemetery to the streets, returning once again to the familiar.

Heavy tiredness enveloped all of her senses and Lee slept for eighteen hours after her discovery. Endless inquiries to the village shopkeepers only resulted in their denial and even more confusion. Mysteriously, the elusive elderly informant from the marketplace had disappeared.

Lee finally gave up and decided not to push her luck. She certainly almost had a *very* real taste of this exotic religion, a taste which may have lost her a career, and more importantly, her life.

Chapter 5
Australia

One long afternoon, an incident which occurred at the airport in Sydney, Australia, resulted in Lee's involvement in an international jewel theft.

Aunt Lee and I had spent our usual vacation week together in her New York City townhouse. The last day before I boarded the bus back to school, Lee received a special delivery from her editor. In the package were travel tickets and an itinerary for the following day. Lee's next travel assignment was in the faraway continent of Australia. All I could think of were kangaroos and *"shrimp on the barbie."* She assured me there were more interesting sites to see than just jumping animals and food, aboriginal colonies and opal mines were only two of the exciting things she mentioned.

Early morning the next day we said our good-byes and made our yearly promises of faithful correspondence. There was no need for the ritual, for we both always kept each other aware of our separate comings and goings.

Lee waited for the final moment and waved as we turned around the last block towards the Interstate. This gave her one hour to return home and grab her luggage for the very long plane ride. She didn't mind rushing though, for she would have lots of time to rest on the trip. Matthew, her houseman and driver, had the car all ready in front of the townhouse for the short ride to John F. Kennedy Airport. Last minute checks to an answering machine assured her that all systems were go.

The tedious trip was extended due to landing difficulties. One of the landing wheels had blown, and no one could disembark until the plane was stable and mechanically sound. Planes were arriving and leaving all around them, but the passengers in the crippled jet were forced to endure the wait. The Captain had turned on the loudspeaker so everyone could check connecting flights. Lee vaguely remembered hearing that one flight was about to leave for the U.S. at roughly the same time she was arriving in Australia. Tempers flared as the temperature in the cabin rose slightly. A pause in the arrival and departure information allowed the Captain to finally announce that the doors would soon open for the passengers to disembark. Cheers and sighs of relief were heard throughout the cabin. Lee was in first class, so she had the privilege of being one of the first to leave the jet.

The next disappointment occurred in the terminal. An announcement was broadcast about the disabling of metal detectors, thus passengers were advised to be patient as individual baggage checks were performed. Thorough luggage and personal checks were enacted on every person coming and leaving the terminal.

Lee retrieved her luggage from the baggage carousel and joined the first available line. As the terminal was very crowded, people were jostling each other constantly. Lee thought nothing of it when a man bumped into her, almost knocking her over her bags. She steadied herself and had just enough time to observe the man's physical appearance. His complexion was swarthy and his hair unkempt, a wrinkled tan raincoat billowed over an equally wrinkled wool suit. Lee probably would not have even paid any attention to him if his personal hygiene had not been so offensive. This alone placed his appearance deep into her memory. However, this was even furthered by the fact that one of his large front teeth was solid gold.

The man murmured his excuses and quickly ran towards the exit. Lee just shrugged her shoulders and moved forward in the line. A full hour later, she hiked her bags up on the checkout counter and hoisted her purse onto her shoulder. The attendant motioned to the purse and Lee laid it on top of her bags. The clerks were quick and thorough in their checks, Lee was quickly asked a few routine customs questions. Assuring that she had no firearms, bombs, or agricultural products going into the country, Lee proceeded to retrieve her bags, closing and locking them.

Not paying much attention to the attendants, Lee reached for her purse when the clerk loudly advised her to "STOP!" One quick snap of the fingers and airport security soon appeared. At least five uniformed members of Sydney's finest came out of the woodwork. Lee's purse was confiscated, as were her passport and driver's license. The officers of the law escorted her to a secure area and began questioning her further.

"Name, address, and reason for visit?" they asked rapidly. "Are you aware of international laws that apply to theft?" they bellowed. "Do you know the penalty for aiding and abetting a crime?" she heard. Lee didn't even have time to think, never mind answer their questions. She had absolutely no idea what this was all about. However she was soon enlightened.

In a private, windowless room, the police inspector began his interrogation by removing a towel-wrapped object from his coat pocket. He unwrapped the towel and presented the most exquisite opal gemstone Lee had ever seen. Fire and ice came to mind as the colors exploded from the stone when he gently rocked the jewel in his hand. It covered his entire palm and exuded prisms of light with each turn. Lee gasped, "Oh, that is the most beautiful opal I have ever seen. But why are you showing it to me when it should be in a museum, or gem shop?" The gentleman was confused, as Lee's surprise and concern seemed genuine. Her surprise was even greater when he told her that the gemstone had been found in her purse! The customs' attendant had also said, "She tried to hide the purse from being checked by putting it on her shoulder." Lee explained that this was an involuntary movement, because she needed two hands to retrieve her two other bags. She didn't even consider that anything contraband would be found, because she had nothing to hide! Lee's honesty was conveyed to her interrogators and the chief inspector asked her to retrace her steps from the plane.

MARIE THERESE

Rapidly rethinking the situation, Lee could not recall any point during her disembarkment when she was without her purse. She backtracked carefully, but kept coming up with nothing. Finally the solution surfaced.

"Hold it, gentlemen," Lee said. "Now I remember an incident. In fact, it must be the incident at which this terrible mishap occurred," she continued. "Standing in line waiting behind the Customs' table, I was rudely jostled by a strange, vile smelling man with a tan wrinkled raincoat," she offered. The Inspector nodded, and Lee went on to describe the gold tooth. With this exclamation, he jumped up from his seat and immediately reached for the telephone. Lee was ushered out to another room and offered libation.

A short time later, Lee heard shouts and the door to the holding room swung open. Two policemen and the Inspector were surrounding the handcuffed culprit with the gold tooth and odoriferous personage. Lee shouted, "Yes, that's him! That's the man who bumped into me in the terminal!"

The police hurried the thief to the inner room and Lee waited outside impatiently. Allowed to use the phone, she called the hotel and notified them of her late arrival, as she didn't want to lose her reservations over this quandary.

Finally the Inspector came out of the inner room, smiling from ear to ear. Lee had been the unknowing participant in a well-stage international jewel theft. The smelly man had confessed the entire plot in less than 10 minutes. The plan went as follows: the thief was to arrive at the terminal; deliberately jostle a passenger on one of the arrival lines depositing the opal in her purse; and then he would depart the country for the U.S.. His partner in crime would perform exactly the same assault when the chosen passenger left the terminal.

Only the partner would retrieve the jewel this time and mail it to a specific address in the U.S.. This plan would confuse anyone following the main thief and make the plan complicated to discover.

However, the thieves had underestimated the capability of the Sydney police. The unsavory man with the gold tooth had been observed by a hidden camera as he surreptitiously performed the heist. A plain-clothes man had secretly planted a small tracking device directly on the culprit's shoulder as he passed on the street. He was followed to the airport and passed through the customs' check. This puzzled the airport guards, and encouraged them to watch him more closely. They had silently observed all of his actions, including the bumping of Lee, and waited patiently for his slip-up.

Meanwhile, the crook's partner had been followed and captured. The shock was so great that he confessed with great emotion. His fear of deportation back to the U.S., where he was wanted for various crimes, overcame his loyalty to his partner. He even shouted out apologies to Lee during the interrogation.

Tired and exasperated, Lee was escorted to her hotel in the Inspector's car. He apologized profusely for her inconvenience and offered her dinner as compensation. Lee accepted gracefully. During dinner, Lee learned that the Inspector's family was the original owner of an opal mine which produced some of the best quality stones in the country. She was even offered a private tour of the operations, with the Inspector as her guide, of course.

Since this incident, Lee has shied away from wearing her lovely opal earrings, a present from the Australian consulate. While their beauty was undeniable, the way she acquired them was less than ideal.

Chapter 6
Monaco

The Principality of Monaco extended an invitation to Aunt Lee and several other travel experts during the week of the Monte Carlo Grand Prix auto race. The aristocracy wanted to increase the tourist population and offer attractive vacation packages to susceptible patrons. No expense was spared to introduce the visitors to all facets of this tiny, but historic country. Little did Lee know that research for an article would be intertwined with foreign intrigue and deception.

A private jet transported the group of journalists on a glamorous flight. Smooth air currents and excellent libation kept the passengers content and eager. Stretch limousines were waiting at the airport to shuttle the group to the famous "Louis XV" restaurant for an early repast. After the group enjoyed haute cuisine, the limousines were summoned to take all of them to the Hotel de Paris, a superb establishment modeled after the Grand Hotel on the Boulevard des Capucines in Paris, France.

Lee's limo companion was a tall, slim gentleman named Peter Rand, who reminded her of James Bond. He was impeccably dressed in a navy Brooks Brothers suit and an Armani silk tie. Faint blue silk threads in his shirt matched the azure hues of the tie. His thick white hair and mustache complimented his handsome face and vivid, tourmaline colored eyes.

A solid gold signet ring with the initial "P" encircled the ring finger of his right hand. The center of the "P" held a magnificent garnet, so multifaceted that it seemed to emit fireworks.

Lee was totally impressed with the man's appearance and demeanor. A faint, unidentifiable accent accompanied eloquent diction as he briefly introduced himself.

A seasoned journalist, Lee preferred to offer good listening skills to new acquaintances, but this man somehow re-directed her interest in his background back to information about herself. She was aware of a very discrete method of diversion exerted by her companion. A warning flag raised in her mind, but she dismissed it as an act of overactive imagination and two glasses of Dom Perignon.

Interestingly, Peter Rand sensed her mistrust and immediately changed his tactic to one of complimentary admiration of her writings. He invited her to join him for a late night supper and perusal of the casino. His charm won her over and the date was confirmed.

The countryside was breathtaking. Estates and ancient stonework were sprinkled sporadically between the majestic French Alps and the Mediterranean Sea. The Oceanographic Museum highlighted the work of Jacques Cousteau on the way to Prince Rainier's Palace. A comprehensive tour was planned for another day, when the select group of tourists was rested from their travel.

Fragrant gardens pre-empted the Hotel de Paris. Baggage was unloaded and golden room keys were distributed. Weary, and slightly tipsy, Lee retired to an elegant suite surely fit for any member of the House of Grimaldi, the princely family of Monaco. A basket of fresh fruits accompanied chilled wine and Perrier on the sideboard. Softly playing Vivaldi created a restful atmosphere amidst the luxurious furnishings. A bowl of roses, in shades of delicate pink graduating to deep purple, was placed on the Louis XV table by the bed. Lee layed down to rest while the fragrance of the roses and the calming music, lulled her senses into peaceful submission. She allowed herself to fall into a deep, restful sleep.

Two hours later, Lee was awoken by muted chimes, refreshed and ready to explore. A large, claw-footed bathtub summoned her. Tiny vials of bath oils and scents further enhanced the ambiance. Lee was already convinced that this was the perfect place for rest and relaxation, a true vacation paradise.

Wrapped in a fluffy, terrycloth robe, Lee was brought back to reality by the chimes again, announcing a telephone call. She answered, and was greeted by her editor.

"Lee," he shouted. "Can you hear me?" "Of course I can hear you Ed, you're perfectly clear," Lee answered. The conversation was brief, but shocking to Lee. Her boss had called to warn her that a rumor was circulating among travel circles that an international band of counterfeiters had aroused the suspicions of the French Gendarmes. The possibility of Monte Carlo as a destination of this band of classy thieves was evident. All questionable visitors could expect interrogation and surveillance.

Lee responded thankfully to her boss and was moved by his concern for her. They had worked together for many years, and his fatherly intentions touched her deeply. She smiled and began her preparations for the evening.

Forewarned about the mode of dress expected in the "high-rollers" section of the casino, Lee extracted a lovely full length, evening sheath of royal blue silk from her walk-in closet. Sapphire earrings and a matching choker completed the ensemble. Strappy satin sandals encased tiny, pedicured feet. Delicate tendrils fell around her face, while the remainder of her curls were gracefully swept up in a feminine style reminiscent of the Gibson girl. Lee knew, from former admirers, that this fashion was very flattering on her. Expert makeup and a quick touch up to her manicure created a very pleasing image in the antique floor mirror. While applying a last minute mist of Chanel no. 5, Lee heard the chimes once more. The caller was Peter Rand, inquiring if she was ready to meet in the Grand Salon. She was.

Peter was openly appreciative of Lee's efforts, kissed her hand, and protectively placed her arm over his own. He was clearly proud to be the escort of such a formidable and lovely woman. Reservations provided them with a table facing the gardens, assuredly a choice location. Candles, wine and light conversation added to an atmosphere of grandeur.

The hours sped quickly by and the couple was anxious to continue the evening observing and perhaps indulging in some games of chance at the casino. Lee was a conservative gambler, but Peter seemed to be quite the experienced risk taker in this type of adventure. His bankroll seemed to replenish itself repeatedly, as he tried his luck at roulette, chemin de fer and blackjack. The high stakes provided incentive, so champagne and hors d'oeuvres appeared with regularity during the games.

Lee was not only mesmerized by the expertise Peter exhibited while in play, but in his endless supply of banknotes. One oddity which didn't escape her notice was Peter's constant habit of depositing his winnings in his inner jacket pocket, and retrieving his betting money from a pocket in his trousers. She dismissed this as a possible "good luck" ritual, the various types of which were common to all gamblers. Some say prayers, repeat chants, mumble curses, and shout promises in their quest for fortune. But once again, Lee's little cautionary flag rose in her brain. She squelched the sensation, again blaming it on the juice of the grape.

The wee hours of the morning came quickly and although Peter was still winning profusely, Lee begged him to excuse her. However, he insisted on cashing in his chips and escorting her back to the hotel. Another feather-like fingertip kiss accompanied a request for a brunch date. Lee assented and floated dreamily in the elevator up to her floor. The massive canopy bed had been turned down and a luscious square of Godiva chocolate lay on her pillow. She had no need for this confection to produce sweet dreams, they were inevitable.

Frowning slightly, Lee could not imagine how chimes had invaded her romantic dream. Then awareness set in. She realized it was the telephone. "Madame, please forgive this unpardonable intrusion," the voice said. "But this is the Hotel Security, and we have reason to believe you are the unknowing accomplice of a crime. Please be prepared to answer a few questions, which will undoubtedly renounce any implication in the incident. An officer will arrive at your room in approximately fifteen minutes to escort you to our Security

Department," he continued. "Again, Madame, our apologies for any inconvenience. Your references and reputation are impeccable, but we feel these same attributes have caused another to compromise you." The conversation was ended.

Hasty dressing and modest repairs to her coiffure were completed just as a knock was heard from the door to the suite. Expecting a uniformed representative of the police, Lee was surprised to be greeted by a doorman, holding a massive bouquet of exquisite white roses. She accepted the delivery and removed the card from among the stems.

The card read: *"My lovely companion, these ambassadors of peace come to you in anticipation of the inconvenience I am soon to inflict on you. In advance, please accept my apologies for whatever troubles occur due to our brief encounter tonight. When the puzzle is solved, I will be many miles away from this magical place and your enchanting presence. But the memory of you and our hours together will forever linger in my thoughts and dreams. Your everlasting friend, Peter Rand."*

Lee's concentration was interrupted by another knock on the door. She quickly hid the card and placed the fragrant blossoms on the bureau.

She opened the door and a voice bellowed out, "Good morning, Madame, I am Captain Fontine, representative of the principality of Monaco. Please forgive the hour of our arrival, but it is of the utmost importance that we discuss a most inopportune situation which involves you." He slid past Lee and quickly surveyed the suite, mentally taking inventory of its contents (including the flowers).

Lee closed the door and after offering the captain a seat, sat in a delicate silk boudoir chair by the fire. Her instincts heightened as she proceeded to reverse the interrogation and learn what this intrusion was about.

"Captain Fontine," she queried, "am I to assume that I am under investigation for an alleged crime?" "If so," she continued, "please get to the heart of the matter and let me know what this is all about?"

The Captain nodded his head and spoke. "Madame, you were observed last evening in the company of Mr. Peter Rand at the casino. Is this true?" he asked.

"Certainly, captain. I was not aware that it is a crime for two adults to enjoy each other's company without notifying the local police!" She stated emphatically. "Now, just what is the problem?"

"Madame," he began, "it is with great regret that I must inform you of a terrible situation in which you have been unknowingly involved. Mr. Peter Rand has been confirmed just two hours ago as an international thief, with connections to the unsavory occupation of counterfeiting. While you were enjoying a seemingly innocent evening encounter with a charming gentleman, just the opposite was true, he used your lovely appearance and irreproachable credentials to surreptitiously exchange counterfeit money for genuine currency at our gaming tables! His betting currency was fake, but his winnings were real!

He has swiftly separated our country from huge sums of cash!"

Lee must have paled in appearance, because the Captain immediately poured her some ice water from the cut glass pitcher.

"Captain," Lee began when she regained her composure, "I assure you, that I too have been duped by this expert con-man. However, I am sure that you are telling me the truth, for just prior to your arrival I received these flowers and this accompanying card."

The Captain read the card and smiled faintly. "Yes, my dear, "he gently spoke, "we have both been duped by an expert in this matter. Monsieur Rand is the top of his profession, and just as much a rogue. He will use anyone, and anything to attain his goal." He went on, "we know him well, and will someday catch him at his antics. However it is too bad you have received such a bad taste of our beautiful country this way. I hope this incident will not cloud your opinion of Monaco or of its inhabitants. As a man, I apologize on behalf of my own gender. Who would dare use so lovely a woman for his ill gotten gain?"

Lee smiled and graciously accepted his apology. She followed the captain to the door of the suite and thanked him for his kind consideration. He performed the traditional French compliment of kissing her hand, and exited to the hallway.

Lee sighed, removed her robe and slid back between the silk sheets to resume her badly needed rest. Exhaustion overcame disappointment and soon welcome sleep performed its healing powers to both body and mind.

What seemed like minutes was really hours later when the familiar chimes once again disturbed Lee's sleep. Confusion caused her to reach out wildly and knock over the European style phone. Suddenly awake, she quickly retrieved the receiver before it pummeled to the floor beside her bed.

"Hello, hello," she shouted. "Hello to you too," said the male voice on the other side of the conversation. Lee sat up straight and swung her legs over the side of the bed as she registered her recognition of the caller. It was Peter Rand.

"Before you say another word, listen and please don't hang up," he begged. "Did you receive my token of apology?"

"Where are you calling from? And do you know what trouble you've caused me?" Lee shouted. "But, I guess you do, or you wouldn't be wherever you are!"

"I just couldn't leave without hearing your voice one more time, and of course to make sure you were safe and uninvolved. I may be a thief, but I am also a gentleman who would never, never leave a lady in permanent distress. Once again, please forgive me for any indiscretions I may have committed, and know that I truly enjoyed the time we spent together. You are the most charming, lovely woman I have ever met, and if the circumstances were different, perhaps we would still be together. But one never knows what the future brings. I never lose hope. Au revoir, ma cherie!" The phone clicked dead.

Fully awake, Lee searched for her notebook and pen and jotted down the beginnings of her article. Always a professional, she dressed quickly, and enjoyed the prescribed tours and local attractions readily available for culture starved tourists. She knew she could write an article filled with passion that would lure vacationers to a tiny land of romance, mystery and history.

For years after the Monaco article was published, sporadic deliveries of white roses would arrive at her home, to her delight. Since prisons do not usually contain florists, she knew that Peter Rand was still the elusive international rogue she had enjoyed so thoroughly.

Chapter 7
Turkey

When thinking about Turkey's famous oriental rug trade, a scene from an old "Cleopatra" movie comes to mind, in which Cleopatra is unceremoniously rolled out of a beautiful oriental rug. Her precocious intention was not the gift of a lovely floor covering, but rather the gift of herself to the royal receiver.

My aunt's involvement with an oriental rug, however, became an international incident of equally marked attention.

Lee had been contracted to travel to Turkey, a most exotic country, to interview a famous rug-maker at his palatial estate. The man was the last living heir to an old established family who had rendered their rug-making services to the royalty of the country for hundreds of years dating back to the Ottoman Empire. Unfortunately a genetic defect had slowly withered down the bloodline until this person was alone with his talents.

Sotheby's Auction House had realized the demand for these exquisite carpets, but a detailed history of the patterns and weaves was hard to acquire. Lee's reputation had earned her the privilege of personally interviewing the man and gathering facts for the identification and authentication of Sotheby's acquisitions.

The journey began in Istanbul, the once great capital of three great empires: the Roman, the Byzantine and the Ottoman. Memories of ancient treasures and revered religious history were visible in the graceful minarets and prestigious palaces. Hot springs and healthful Turkish baths availed themselves to tired, weary travelers.

Although the store and warehouse resided in Istanbul, the actual weaving of the rugs occurred in western Anatolia, in a region called Ushak. The original family home, expanded over much time, was still the primary residence of Lee's host, Mr. Azzizi.

Mr. Azzizi had a private limousine collect Lee from the airport in Istanbul; retrieve him at the store, and drive them to his home in Ushak. Along the way, Mr. Azzizi proudly pointed out the many beautiful antiquities and monuments that splendidly ornamented the land. He reinforced Lee's historical knowledge with traditional folktales and religious beliefs. Lee was raptly enchanted by the intense national pride exhibited by her host.

Passing through the countryside, Mr. Azzizi veered the subject of his lecture to the origin of his precious rugs. He pointed to a hillside where plump sheep foraged among the grasses for the sweetest blades to eat. Thick, white wool covered their backs and Mr. Azzizi assured Lee that only the best wool from the back and shoulders of these sheep was shorn, and then hand-spun into yarn for his rugs. He explained that the long fibers of sheep shorn in the spring produced the most preferable wool. Traditional spindles and spinning wheels are the tools used in this region to make the hand-spun wool called Kirman. After the shorn wool is cleaned, dried, teased and combed, the longest fibers are chosen to be hand spun. These wool threads make the skeleton and pile of the rugs.

Hours of driving through lush hillsides later, we reached our destination. An ornate gold painted gate swung open at the request of an automatic door opener. A long driveway snaked its way through exotic topiaries of desert greenery. Flowing fountains, also painted gold, spewed forth cool trickles of recycled water. Mr. Azzizi told Lee he was a conservationist and that the water was continuously recycled throughout the entire estate. Under a portico of sand colored stone, the car stopped and they were discharged to a waiting houseman.

Mr. Azzizi presented Lee to the capable hands of the houseman,

TURKEY

Adam, and stated that he would join her at 7 for dinner. He wished Lee a fine afternoon of rest after the long journey. Lee thanked him for being so thoughtful, and gratefully retired to her room's sumptuous bed (naturally, it was also gold gilded). At around 4 p.m. Lee awoke to the gentle breeze of an overhead fan. A tray with a frosted glass and a pitcher of tangy fruit punch sat on a bombe chest in the corner of the room. The gilt bed was placed on the most luxurious thick carpet delicately shaded in hues of yellow. The soft gauze eggshell colored curtains billowed over the floor-to-ceiling windows, and gently swayed in the artificial breeze. A mosaic design had been painted on the curved ceilings and bordered with gold painted moldings. A dressing table filled with guest powders and scents filled an alcove at the far side of the room. The attached bath was similarly decorated and held shelves of plump, fluffy yellow bath towels. Shampoos, soaps and lotions filled a small vanity complimenting the very modern jacuzzi.

Lee bathed and pampered herself like a princess, also enjoying the sensual feelings of her bare feet on the velvety carpet. Her suitcase had been emptied and her clothes pressed and hung in a large chifferobe. She chose a lovely pink chiffon dress, which complimented her pixie haircut and tanned features. White sandals and a string of pearls with matching earrings were all the adornments she needed. Light makeup completed her look and she was ready for dinner. Mr. Azzizi had agreed to be taped, so she tucked her mini recorder into a small white bag. A note left on her bedside table gave directions to the "garden room" where dinner would be served.

The garden room was actually an indoor re-creation of the beautiful outdoor topiary, complete with fountains. Complimenting the greenery were vases and bowls of fresh cut flowers in perfect stages of bloom. Spicy jasmine mingled with sweet honeysuckle, and roses stood alone boasting their fragile beauty.

Mr. Azzizi welcomed Lee once more to his home and dinner began. As his carpets were his favorite topic of discussion, she was encouraged to turn on the recorder during the meal. Between courses, Lee learned about the trade passed down for generations to Mr. Azzizi. His family's history could be traced back as far as 1471, when Mehmed

II was an Ottoman Sultan who decreed that only Azzizi carpet would adorn his palace. His reign was short, but the tradition of the Azzizi carpets upheld their importance, even until present day.

About half way through the meal (of 11 courses) Lee realized that Mr. Azzizi was tiring of talk, so she proceeded to compliment him on his carpets, his home, and especially the decorating of the guestroom. Lee told him that she was so comfortable that it felt like she had chosen the patterns and colors herself. She expressed special enjoyment of the carpet, both to the eyes and to the feet. Mr. Azzizi beamed with pride.

When Lee felt she had sufficiently assured him of her pleasure, he put his hand up in supplication. He stood up, bowed, and said, "I am so pleased with your respectful interview, Lee, that I will be honored if you will accept a small token of my appreciation. I will have a similar carpet, in the same hues, sent to your home in the U.S.. After it arrives, every day you will remember your friend in Ushak by wiggling your toes on my carpet. I will smile each morning thinking of your enjoyment. Please say you will accept this little gift. It will make an old man very happy." Lee was so surprised and happy that she jumped up and gave him a hug. An everlasting friendship was made that day.

Three days and four tapes later, Lee packed her bags and waved goodbye to her new friend, Mr. Azzizi. She promised to send copies of the magazine piece upon publication. The chauffeur drove her back to the airport in Istanbul for the long plane trip home.

The ride was enjoyable and in her mind Lee went over the backbone of the article she intended to present to her editor. She listened to the tapes and took additional notes, as new memories emmerged. Presently the noise and confusion of the airport blotted out her concentration. The driver had her bags taken directly to the plane and Lee, after thanking him, retreated to the lounge area to wait to board.

A large window allowed Lee to watch the porters loading the baggage onto the plane. She saw suitcases, carriages, and even dogs being herded into the part of the plane which didn't carry human passengers. This sight made Lee remember the gift that Mr. Azzizi had promised. She left the lounge and found the airplane attendant who was in the information booth. A short inquiry assured Lee that it would be loaded into the plane within the half-hour. She went back to the lounge and waited to see the loading. Just as the attendant said, the well-packaged rug was shuttled on a cart to the plane.

Just as the rug passed by the window, a remarkable thing happened. A man dressed in native robes ran up to the cart and screamed while waving at the attendant to stop the cart. Lee could hear him yell, "Stop, thief! That is my rug! Do not put it on that plane!"

Lee grabbed her bag and raced to the exit door and the ramp leading down to the loading section beside the plane. By this time the airport police had arrived and were trying to make sense of this scene. The man continued to scream, "My master, descendant of Suleyman I the Magnificent, is the owner of this carpet. This thief is trying to smuggle it to the U.S., this is an insult!" His anger was apparent and when he dramatically threw up his hands, his robe parted and disclosed a wide belt with a nasty looking dagger in it. Lee wondered how he had passed through the metal detector in the airport lobby.

When Lee arrived at the scene she tried to get the attention of the police officer in charge. "Sir," she shouted, "this is my carpet! It was a gift from Mr. Azzizi, of Ushak. Please contact him and confirm this fact. I have no idea who this man is or why he wants my carpet, but it is mine and I am taking it home with me!"

The officer was distressed, and ordered the carpet to be held in a locked room while he made some inquiries.

Meanwhile, Lee was back waiting in the lounge nervously. A short time later the doors opened and three men, all dressed in native robes, quickly walked over to Lee. One man walked in front, and another took up the rear, as the second approached Lee. The middle man spoke to Lee, while expertly hiding her fear she exhibited a countenance of cool control.

"Excuse me, madame," he said. "Please let me introduce myself. I am Aman Fortiz, Emir of Oman. I, too, am traveling to the U.S. and have purchased an exquisite carpet from Mr. Azzizi to take to my penthouse in Manhattan. My bodyguard was quite distressed when he saw your name and address on the carpet with the famous Azzizi packaging seal. He had no idea that TWO Azzizi carpets would be travelling to New York. His thought was that the carpet was purposely mismarked and would be mistaken in U.S. Customs. You can understand his concern for the potential loss." Mr. Fortiz offered his hand in friendship and continued to speak, "as an apology for your inconvenience, would you please do me the honor of accompanying me in my first class cabin on the plane, and we can discuss our common enjoyment of beautiful floor coverings? Wonderful conversation will accompany an excellent meal, of course."

Lee was enchanted by this exotic, and very handsome, man. She acknowledged and accepted his generous offer with a charming smile. What a perfect way to end her story for Sotheby's with the comments of a satisfied customer.

Chapter 8
Martha's Vineyard

The inheritance of an elegant scrimshaw pendant prompted Lee to propose a trip to Martha's Vineyard, a ferry ride away from Cape Cod, Massachusetts. Not only was this beautiful place chock full of history and tradition, but it was also a favorite travel destination of vacationers far and wide.

Property availability was at a premium in this vintage place; inhabitants tended to keep real estate within family limits, rarely allowing land to be acquired by outsiders. Although the year-round inhabitants are small in number, the tourist population is phenomenally large. Along the shore the homes are largely Victorian in style, many of them refurbished whaling captain's homes. Their location afforded the waiting wives and children of yore a distant view of their leaving or returning husbands, fathers and sons.

A favorite architectural adornment of the spacious homes is the widow's walk, a railed roof top gallery designed to observe vessels at sea. A known pastime of the whaling captain's wife was to pace patiently around this walk, searching the seas for her husband's ship. Not only was the whaling occupation dangerous, it did not accommodate timetables; a crew could be gone from home for years at a time, searching and capturing their precious cargo. When slaughtered, the whales were dissected and prepared right on the ship for resale upon return. Unsavory or unsalable parts were discarded, and the decks cleaned and prepared for the next conquest. Only then did the ships return to port.

After the chase, the capture, the kill and dissection of the whale, there was ample time for sailors to rest and carve scrimshaw. This art entailed the use of small pieces of whalebone, or ivory, which was carved into beautiful jewelry and artifacts. The natural graining of the bone would serve as the base of the design, varying with the imagination of the carver.

Lee's pendant was carved in the front with two deeply etched roses. The detail was so complete that one could almost see the dew on the petals. The normally smooth backing of the oval piece of jewelry had a heart carved on it with the initials "TM" above an ampersand in the middle, and the initials "AD" on the bottom. The year 1656 could be seen with the aid of a magnifying glass on the very edge of the ivory. A tiny hole had been carved out of the top, just wide enough for delicate velvet ribbon to be inserted. Encircling the hole were exquisitely carved leaves.

The person who willed Lee the pendant had lived in Edgartown. Her name was Mary Daggett, and she descended from some original settlers who held whaling as their trade. As one of the initials on the pendant was a "D", Lee was sure that there was a romantic tale attached to this legacy. She intended to do some digging both in the library at Edgartown, and among the townsfolk who may have been related to Mary Daggett. Little did Lee know that this pendant would surface one of the most famous true stories passed down through the generations of Martha's Vineyard society.

The elder Thomas Mayhew was one of the founding fathers of Martha's Vineyard and set foot on the shores in roughly 1642. Land titles were divided up amongst the first settlers and names were chosen for the parcels of land. These settlers were busy clearing land, building homes, tilling the soil and fishing. One John Daggett Senior was mentioned in the annals as assigned 500 acres of land adjoining the Senior Mayhew property. There seemed to have been a feud brewing between the elders Mayhew and Daggett, as mention is made of Governor Mayhew not honoring the early assignation of specific land parcels to Daggett. The long lasting fight between neighbors culminated in a court fight, which Daggett won. The family problems between the Mayhews continued even after Daggett died, when Mayhew had a proviso added to his will concerning the limits of Daggett's land ownings.

Thomas Mayhew's eldest son, also named Thomas, grew up hating the farm. He was an independent boy who loved freedom and detested regimental chores and monotonous duties, both of which farming was all about. As first-born, he was expected to carry on the family name and business, which was farming. From his early years he would sneak away from the pastures and wander along the fierce Atlantic coastline. He collected shells and bits of driftwood and debris coughed up from the sea. Storms thrilled him and his happiest moments were spent watching whaling ships arrive and depart from the shores. His mother sheltered her boy, but found it difficult dealing with his discontent of the elder Mayhew. Luckily, Luke, their second son, had the opposite temperament as the young Thomas, and worshiped farming and animals. As long as the chores were not neglected and the farm crop produced, there was little conflict. This was due largely to the tactful management of Mrs. Mayhew.

John Daggett, Thomas Mayhew's nemesis, also had a son the same age as the younger Thomas. He, like the second Mayhew son, took great pleasure growing things and hunting. However, the second child of John Daggett closer resembled young Thomas. She was a girl named Alicia. Although dutiful and helpful with chores around the Daggett farm, she preferred sitting by the shore, using charcoal on parchment to capture the beauty of breaking waves and passing ships. Gulls gave her music and she delighted in watching sea creatures dance upon the shores when the tide went out.

Fate brought these two young naturalists together on the Vineyard shores many times. Strict religious upbringing made them both shy, although eager to share experiences. Time helped to bridge the gap between them and a fast friendship ensued. They frolicked, gathered shells, named clouds, and swapped fish stories between them. Days passed into years and maturing senses turned the friendship into budding love. However, due to the family feud, the couple still met in secrecy.

By the time young Thomas Mayhew was sixteen, his father gave up the quest to make him a farmer. Gentle insistence from his wife and the success of his second son urged him to allow the boy to pursue the adventurous life of a whaler. The elder Mayhew allowed Thomas to sign on with a ship as an apprentice to learn the trade. Mrs. Mayhew wept profusely as she waved to her first-born, leaving on this most dangerous activity. Unbeknownst to the elder Mayhews, another person stood on the sandy beach and waved most emphatically, shifting a white linen hankie back and forth from hand to hand as a signal. This was of course, Alicia Daggett.

Thomas' first day on the ship was both wonderful and trying. Every muscle and bone ached as he learned the "ropes" of sailing. There were knots to learn, sails to open and close, decks to swab, and methods on how to retain the contents of your stomach under rough waters. Seasoned sailors were a hardy, but cantankerous group, who loved nothing more than to torment any new recruits. Thomas learned many, many lessons on his trial run.

Getting out to the whales was difficult enough, but when the sightings began and the hunt ensued, a whole new episode began in the chronicles of whaling.

On- the-job-training was the method of teaching, and if the harsh lessons were not properly learned one could possibly lose a limb or a life. Luckily years of forced farm chores had toughened up Thomas, but this new life was both a physical and mental strain. He knew he had chosen the right path when the first sighting of a full-grown whale was reported. His adrenaline pumped and he dug into his chores like a seasoned old salt of a sailor. The chase was a breathtaking experience, and the capture and kill was both barbaric and satisfying.

The captain allowed a few hours after the kill for the men to catch their breaths and rest their limbs before they had to begin the arduous duty of cutting up the carcass, and picking out the parts of the whale that were good for sale while discarding the rest back into the sea. Food and drink were passed around, and sailors sang and danced around on the deck.

After months of sailing, with lots of physical labor and burning sun and tropical rains, Thomas noticed subtle changes about his person.

His limbs were brown in color and muscular in form. The childish puffiness of his cheeks had melted away and fine chiseled cheekbones erupted just under his skin. Even a sparse stubble of a beard was visibly apparent on his face.

Thomas was pleased about the changes and wondered if his mother would approve. During a moment of loneliness he even allowed his mind to wander back to the shores of Martha's Vineyard, and the white handkerchief that he last saw waving on the shore.

The backbreaking and unctuous job of carving up the dead whale was enough to clear his brain of any sensitive thoughts. Blood was ankle deep on the decks and blubber and intestines were distastefully strewed all over the place. As the discarded parts of the whale were instantly thrown overboard, sharks swam freely around the ship, gorging themselves. The good parts of the whale were expertly cut up and packaged in wooden barrels to be stored below the decks. Methods were preformed to prevent rancidity and rot. The job was disgusting at best, and down right sickening at worst. Young Thomas lost his own stomach contents many times during the ordeal. The old sailors heartily enjoyed this seasoning of the new apprentice. Only his strong will and determination to survive allowed Thomas to surge on with his duties.

However, the dissection of the whales was not the only arduous task. Following the operation the whole ship had to be thoroughly cleaned of all whale debris. Careful cleanliness prevented horrible infections and illnesses contracted through filthy conditions. A good captain was reputed for being clean. This also guaranteed him a good crew who would be healthy and alive for the next expedition.

With the dissection, storing and cleaning done, the sailors could relax for the long journey back to civilization. During this time they sang songs, learned to dance, wrote journals, and carved scrimshaw. Thomas found one of the seasoned sailors who was an expert carver and eager to share his talent. The choicest pieces of discarded whalebone were kept by the sailors for just this purpose. Thomas found that he too had a hidden talent to bring out the beauty of the bone with carvings. Surely the memory of Alicia Daggett inspired his creativity. The memory of a discovered wild rose bush not far from their favorite meeting place inspired him to etch the likenesses of the roses onto an oval piece of bone. Polishing brought out smoothness to the back of the piece and he punched a small hole at the very top of the oval. The roses were so lifelike that he could almost smell their scent when he allowed his imagination to soar. Tiny, sculptured leaves surrounded the beautiful artifact. Finally, Thomas carved a delicate heart on the reverse side of the pendant and inscribed the initials "TM & AD." In minute numbers he added the year. Thomas found a small, clean piece of oilcloth and wrapped the pendant carefully. He tucked it into his duffle bag and slept, dreaming of Alicia and the seashore.

Edgartown shore bore the footprints of Alicia Daggett every day until the rising tide washed them away with the seaweed. She strained her eyes and climbed the highest rock ledges to try and see the returning ship. Day after day she returned home, sad and disappointed. She wrote in her journal and recorded every meeting she and Thomas had enjoyed, from early childhood through the present. She treasured every colorful shell and piece of driftwood that Thomas had given her. Farm chores were completed hurriedly to ensure ample time to raise her easel and sketch seascapes as she held her vigil.

A year and a half later, Alicia's dream came true when she saw the huge billowing white sails of the whaling ship in the distant horizon. She hurried back to the farm with her sketching tools and smoothed her frock with one hand while brushing her chestnut curls with the other. Sea winds had colored her cheeks so no pinching would she necessary. She bit her lips to make them bright.

She knew exactly how much time it would take for the ship to get to the harbor. Months and months of watching at the shore made her an expert of sea space and time. Allowing herself ample time to get to the wharf, she set out on the quick journey.

Alicia arrived at the dock to see the whaler being tied up and secured. Then the barrels and bundles of whale cargo were unloaded and watched by weapon bearing guards. Just as her heart was about to burst with anticipation, the crew began disembarking. Propriety insisted that Alicia stay back away from the dock, but she slowly inched closer as the sailors walked down the wooden plank. Each had a large duffle bag on their shoulder and it was hard to discern one from the other. She shielded her eyes from the sun and scrutinized each body that arrived. Fear and frustration were about to make her cry when she suddenly felt a tap on her shoulder. A quick turn had her face to face with a tanned, bearded fellow. A shout of surprise escaped from her lips as she realized that this was indeed her beloved Thomas, changed though he was. They embraced openly and words were replaced by hugs and kisses. Thomas handed Alicia the oilcloth packet and she hastened to open it. Her exclaimations of joy when she saw the elegant object of his affection were all he needed to hear. Alicia hunted in her pockets and found a thin ribbon of velvet, which she worked through the hole on the top of the pendant. Thomas helped her by tying it loosely around her throat. She vowed to wear it every day of her life.

Thomas's mother had surreptitiously noticed the budding relationship between Alicia and Thomas. She kept the secret from the elder Thomas, and vowed to help the young couple enjoy their union. Upon his return, Thomas found a quiet moment to tell his mother of his intentions to wed Alicia and asked for her blessing. A clandestine meeting with Alicia's mother had ensured that both women would help their children in dealing with their fathers, so Thomas and Alicia were at least assured some support.

However, both of the stubborn fathers absolutely refused to accept the merging of their two families. The feud was still very much alive and bad feelings abounded. More time went by and the young lovers decided to elope. They found a sympathetic sea captain who officiated the ceremony and blessed their union. A meeting with their parents didn't ease the tensions, so the newlyweds left both of their family's farms and found a cottage by the sea. Young Thomas was thrifty and had saved all of his sea bounty. Soon he bought a weather bitten but large mansion that sat on a hill facing the sea. They lived in the cottage and spent all of their free time making the mansion comfortable. However, the mansion was cursed, as an unexpected tragedy had occurred to each of the families who resided there, but Thomas and Alicia were not superstitious and were determined to make this Victorian relic a safe and happy home.

The renovation was just about complete when Thomas was called to go out on a Whaling expedition. Whales were sighted in abundance and time could not be wasted. Two days notice was all he had to secure his new home and wife with provisions and safe surroundings.

Their parting was sad, and Alicia vowed to think of Thomas every day. She also vowed to watch for his ship from the widow's walk. Every day, townsfolk could look up towards the mansion and watch her lonely vigil. Luckily, the couple had been blessed with the birth of a daughter, Emily, two months before her father left. Emily would lie in Alicia's arms and hold the whalebone pendant for hours. It seemed to have an eerie, soothing effect on the baby girl.

Although the older Mayhew had forbidden any contact between the other members of the family and the younger Thomas Mayhews, Thomas's mother often made secret visits to her daughter-in-law and granddaughter.

A very hard winter came and went, and spring still brought no news of the whaling ship and its crew. Storms took their toll on the land and farm crops were late in planting. The Thomas mansion withstood the rough weather, and Thomas's mother had sent over her younger son to help with cutting wood for fuel. He was sworn to secrecy and never did reveal his participation in the activity. The senior Thomas wife also sent provisions when she thought Alicia or the baby might be in need.

Emily was over a year old, and still took comfort in stroking the smooth, cool stone around her mother's neck. It was almost as if this link to her father gave her peace.

Finally, one crisp fall day, Alicia trekked up the winding stairs to the walk with Emily. They both bundled up as the sea winds whipped around the top of the mansion unmercifully. Huddling together while drinking warm tea, they both shouted at the same time when a huge sail came into view. The sea was choppy and the sloop was rocking hard against the rough waves. But it persevered on its quest to get the cargo to shore.

Reversing down the winding stairs, Alicia and Emily prepared to go to the dock to meet Thomas. As this was the first ship to arrive in many months, the dock was full of people waiting for the arrival. In due time the ship docked, once again Alicia watched as precious cargo was unloaded and guarded. This time she was prepared for any physical change in Thomas. However, when the crew disembarked, she didn't recognize any of them. Her heart beating wildly, she watched as the last member of the crew, the Captain, left the ship. Pushing and shoving, with Emily well protected, Alicia made her way to the ship's chief. A bad premonition seemed to make her feet drag.

The Captain, a large bearded man with a tricorn hat, saw the woman and child and knew exactly who they were. He took Alicia's arm and steered her to an unoccupied area of the dock. The story he told was one of uncommon valor and heroism. The whaling expedition was the most dangerous he had ever commandeered, a great white whale gave them a difficult chase and had done considerable damage to the ship. During the capture, the panicked mammal plunged downward to the sea, dragging several harpooners with him. Thomas heroically threw himself into the water and grabbed the harpooner's rope, rescueing the fellow just before he was drowned. However, the rope suddenly looped up and encircled Thomas's neck, breaking it upon impact. He had an honorable burial at sea and was given a posthumous Medal of Honor.

Alicia paled and weakened at the knees, but she held on steadily to Emily.

The Captain supported them both and brought forth some brandy for Alicia to sip. He asked to accompany her back to her home, and had another shipmate gather Thomas's belongings, which now were hers. Alicia nodded her ascent and they began the sad journey home. The captain carried Thomas's dufflebag over his shoulder, and supported Alicia and Emily with his free arm.

After Thomas's death, Alicia and Emily lived a quiet, but content, life in the mansion on the hill. Alicia continued her vigil on the widow's walk every day of her life. Emily would sometimes join her, but as she grew she knew that this was a special place where her mother could silently be with her father in spirit.

When Alicia knew the end of her life was approaching, she gave Emily the whalebone pendant; she said that Emily would never be alone as long as she had this token of her parent's love. Emily put the pendant around her neck, and she too wore it every day of her life. Emily grew up and one day was walking along the beach when she met a fellow beachcomber. Normally very shy, Emily responded with spirit when the fellow addressed her. A chance encounter soon became an afternoon ritual between the two. Friendship and respect blossomed into love. And history repeated itself, as it all so often does.

    Emily had a daughter, and her daughter repeated the process. The lineage starting with the Thomases and the Daggetts continued until one last female descendent remained. This descendent, Mary Daggett, never married and passed away leaving the whalebone pendant to my Aunt Lee. Lee treasured the inheritance even more now that she knew its history.

Chapter 9
Appalachia

A fact-finding trip to Appalachia became a near disaster one blistering August week.

Lee was sent by her editor to gather research and eventually write about the folklore and family traditions practiced by the close-knit clans in the American mountains of Appalachia. Old wives' tales and rumors about the area needed confirmation from real sources. Hopefully, photographs of this magnificent mountainous countryside and its inhabitants would be permitted.

A good many of the two thousand plus miles of the Appalachian Trail led Lee and her photographer, Dick Modine, deep into the lush forestry of Kentucky. Sources pointed them in this direction for a sampling of the lifestyles of authentic hill people. A reliable four-wheel drive vehicle was rented, and supplies, including sustainability gear, were purchased. Country stores and rural post offices replaced shopping malls, pick-up trucks took the place of compact sedans.

Elliot County was chosen as the focal point of our quest. Characteristics of poverty qualified it as an Appalachian Regional Commission (ARC) Distressed County. With a total population of slightly over 6,500 people, more than 6,000 in 1990 were age 65 and over. This led them to seek information from citizens who had lived a lifetime of precedents which influenced their present. They decided to stop at all of the country stores, churches, and gathering places they could find on their way to Elliot to soak up local gossip and suggestions for their project.

Just before Lee and Dick reached Elliot County, they parked the vehicle at a clearing beside the main road and decided on their method of attack. Hints and suggestions had been amply supplied by the various storekeepers and landowners they had met along the way. It was widely agreed that the most revered person in Elliot County to help them was a septuagenarian named Granny Pickle; she was one of the "Granny Women" who used native plants for food and medicine.

Granny's actual age was debatable, but her memory was sharp. With the exception of electricity, Granny had not permitted any modern renovations to her property since the Great Depression. She had never (to anyone's knowledge) seen a doctor, pharmacist, or taken a single vitamin supplement in all her years. As she kept her cabin warm in the bitter Kentucky winters by firewood only, her stamina could be compared to that of any man in the county. Granny Pickle had never married and thus escaped an early death in childbirth, as was frequently experienced by so many women born in the same age, however she raised numerous foster children who would otherwise be motherless orphans. It was never necessary to supplement her homegrown garden and livestock, consisting of chickens and two pigs, with store-bought goods. Her method of livestock breeding was known only to her and the quality of the meat was superb. Methods of preservation and storage of the food was antiquated, but never dangerous to one's health.

Granny's entire lifestyle mirrored that of her ancestors before her. A heavy wooden shelf, which took up one full wall of the cabin, contained very old books of recipes, remedies, traditions and prayers to help one through all of life's many trials. Granny followed these texts with religious fervor, and the entire county referred to her knowledge to keep them safe and healthy. Payment for her services was made with food, chopped firewood, dry goods, or even family heirlooms (which she found a way to return to the giver).

The last storekeeper they visited gave Lee and Dick detailed directions to Granny Pickle's cabin. He also said, "You needn't worry about being announced, because she already knows you are a-comin!" A mountain dulcimer sent its haunting notes somewhere in his back room, behind the store.

He continued, "You are to stay on the main road, and then make a left at Pop Wilson's. You will recognize Pop sitting in a rocking chair on his front porch humming. A couple of miles later you will see an old split maple by the forked road. Bear to the right of the fork 'til you see three large boulders. The path to Granny Pickle's is right behind the third boulder. A patch of orange tiger lilies will light up the beginning of the path."

"Take care," he warned, "the path is purposely over-grown to discourage trespassers. But, friends are always welcome." He nodded twice, and sat down to whittle.

The main road was suddenly devoid of blacktop about two miles after their last stop. This inhibited their ability to exceed the 15 mph speed limit, but their earlier selection a vehicle with four-wheel-drive was soon to pay off. Ruts and furrows emerged in front of them, and behind them appeared patches of smooth brown earth.

All of a sudden, they heard a strange, off-key sound, which turned out to be the persistent humming of Pop Wilson. Sure enough, there he was rocking in time to the tune he hummed. As instructed, they veered left on to a new road and traveled the couple of miles to the split maple by the fork in the road. Heading down the right fork, they knew they had to find the three boulders as landmarks. Lee and Dick had no idea that these boulders would be mini-mountains of granite! In between each boulder was about one quarter mile of dirt road. As promised, directly after the third boulder they saw the patch of orange tiger lilies announcing the path to Granny Pickle's homestead. They parked the car by the boulder, and each took a backpack with supplies, cameras, and a token gift for Granny.

Lee and Dick had to keep looking down in order to follow the path, for the surrounding foliage was more than simply over-grown. In fact, it was strangling; there were full-grown trees encircled with snaking vines that grabbed at your arms and ankles, making it difficult to walk. Although they both wore jeans, they still felt the brambles and thorns that protected the wild flowers and berries. Heat and sweat performed together to make their clothes sticky and damp. Lee and Dick wore hats, which kept the low branches from tangling their hair, but the sweat poured down their faces and necks. One hand was used to wave away foliage to walk through the path as the other swished away insects from their faces. Fifteen minutes of this exercise and both travelers were exhausted, sweaty and dirty.

Lee suggested a break to reconnoiter, and Dick was quite willing to agree. Each downing a cool bottle of Perrier helped the situation considerably. After quenching her parched throat, Lee climbed up on a "small" boulder of about four feet in height and surveyed the layout of the land. To her surprise, not fifty feet away there was a clearing. Centered squarely in the clearing was a tiny, rustic log cabin spewing out smoke from its chimney.

Wildflowers surrounded the home and a sizeable garden blossomed in the backyard. A pig pen and chicken coop rested on the side of the cabin housing two pigs, six or seven hens and a rooster. The livestock looked healthy and announced Lee and Dick's presence with lively banter. A large, non-descript dog of the hound variety sat on a rag rug directly in front of the screened front door. He didn't moved a muscle, but followed their every step with his large, liquid brown eyes.

They decided to stay about twenty feet away from the front porch and announce themselves. Lee shouted, "Hello, Granny Pickle, I am Lee Farthingale from the travel magazine. May my colleague and I speak to you for a few moments?" Almost instantly a petite figure appeared in the doorway. She opened the screen door and came out on to the porch, directly behind the lounging pooch. "Certainly, certainly .... Welcome to my home," Granny said.

Her hair, as white and soft as the meringue on a pie, fluffy and cloudlike, was wound around into a neat little bun on the nape of her neck. A paisley dress of soft pink, flowing material reached her ankles. Circling a delicate neck was a white tatted collar. Sturdy leather old-fashioned laced boots covered very small feet. A complexion that was clear and wrinkleless complimented the tiniest of noses and enormous dark blue eyes.

A small hand signal to the dog caused him to get up and lumber over to the guests, sniffing and wagging his tail. Granny acknowledged this affirmation, and she beckoned them on in. The dog accompanied them to the porch, and when they were safety inside (with Granny) he took up his post on the rag rug. Lee had never seen more formidable guard.

The inside of Granny's house was just as quaint and hospitable as the outside. Shining wide planked wood floors were covered with colorful area rugs woven from rags. Plump comfortable armchairs and a sofa were adorned and backed with white lacy antimacassars. Worn, earth tone knitted afghans were draped over each chair. Stitched crewel pillows lined the back of the sofa. Neatly tied bunches of herbs and flowers hung from each of the windowsills to dry. Every corner of the room exuded pleasant, spicy smells from the drying foliage. Lee closed her eyes and pictured a pitcher of cool lemonade as the scent of lemon verbena permeated the air.

As if reading Lee's mind, Granny silently retreated to the kitchen and returned with a pitcher of the most delicious lemonade Lee had ever tasted. Bits of the fruit tartly quenched her thirst as she gratefully gulped down the treat. Dick filled his glass three times before a sterm look from Lee advised him to slow down. They offered their hostess a variety of small tins of hard candies, hoping that Granny was not diabetic. She was tickled to receive the licorice, lemon, and butterscotch drops. Lee knew the present was a hit when she immediately opened the first tin and (after offering one to her guests) popped a lemon drop right into her mouth.

Refreshed by the libation, Lee and Dick were invited by Granny into her kitchen, where she concocted all of her potions and cooked her elixirs. This library of herbal ingredients was extensive, and very neatly cataloged on rows of wooden shelves. Mason jars held crushed herbs, leaves and flower petals. Metal boxes contained powders, which Granny had ground with a stoneware mortar and pestle. Everything was marked in block print on white labels. Large and small pots alike hung from long hooks suspended from the exposed ceiling beams. Hand poured beeswax candles hung from their wicks on little hooks fastened to a central post in the kitchen.

A big, black iron stove dominated most of one wall of the kitchen. The smell of roasting chicken made their mouths water and stomachs growl. Potatoes were boiling on top of the stove and the biggest coffeepot Lee had ever seen was percolating away. Another big pot threatened to boil as shucked sweet corn sat on a large serving plate beside it.

The kitchen table was set with blue delft dinnerware and a white linen tablecloth, embroidered with forget-me-nets. A small, squat earthenware vase sat in the middle of the table, bursting with wild purple violets. Churned butter and a pitcher of frothing fresh milk complemented the menu.

To her guests' glee, Granny said, "Hope you folks are hungry! I seem to have cooked a bit too much today!" Helping with preparations, they sat down to the most delicious meal either of them had enjoyed in many days (or perhaps ever)!

After dinner and the clean up of the kitchen, Granny invited Lee and Dick to relax in the parlor while they interviewed her. It was very hard to stay awake after being so aptly satiated.

They inquired about each and every one of Granny's remedies and prevention medicines. She was consulted on a wide variety of diseases, everything ranging from common colds and pneumonia to the chicken pox. Most women of childbearing age conferred with Granny during their pregnancies and after their deliveries. Common sense combined with age-old use of natural medicines proved successful for almost all of her patients. Peppermint tea for indigestion and chamomile tea for colicky babies helped old and young people alike. Herbs to clear congestion and powders for constipation relieved many a sickly visitor to Granny's infirmary. Hot mustard plaster poultices and cold compresses made with herbal contents soothed various aches, pains and sprains. When asked about serious or life-threatening problems, Granny explained that she would make the patient as comfortable as possible, and send someone for professional help. However, she recently gave someone stitches, a logger who had accidentally mistaken his leg for a tree. They met the logger at a later time, and his scar was barely noticeable thanks to Granny.

Intermittently throughout the interview, a knock on the door would produce either a patient or a messenger, sent for help or herbal teas. Ardent respect was observed for Granny's position in the hierarchy. She obviously did not need to worry about social status or political elections.

About an hour into the interview, Lee noticed a strange sensation taking over her body. She felt flushed and had a hard time focusing her eyes due to extremely heavy eyelids. Minor discomfort intensified into an unusual itchy feeling in various locations of her anatomy. Reaching up to scratch her ear, Lee was horrified to feel that her earlobe had swelled up at least three times its normal size! Upon moving her fingers, she experienced numbness and abnormal swelling. Welts appeared all over her hands and her toes were itchy and very tight within her walking boots. A pinkish rash had begun to appear on her face, right above her cheekbones. The rapidly advancing illness, whatever it was, soon took over Lee's senses. She had trouble speaking and her tongue felt large and fuzzy.

Granny, observing the transformation, got up from her rocker and disappeared into the kitchen and out the back door. Dick was frantic and kept asking Lee, "What's happening to you? Where did she go? What can I do for you?" Lee was more concerned for Dick's panic than for her own wellbeing.

Granny soon came rushing back into the parlor with an armful of wildflowers. The stems were bright green and long with lots of tiny leaves. The flowers were a combination of orange and yellow. She washed her hands in brown soap and bade Dick to do the same. Then she directed Lee and Dick to grab handfuls of the wildflowers and crush them, stems and all, until a clear liquid came out. She instructed them to use the sticky liquid as a rub for all the spots on Lee's body that were swollen or rashed. Even a cloth was soaked in the crushed flower liquid and placed over Lee's swollen eyelids. When Dick and Lee were busy following directions, Granny disappeared again and returned with a mug of liquid for Lee to drink.

After the flower bath, Granny made Lee lie down on her featherbed and drew the curtains, hiding the sun. Lee quickly fell asleep and Granny covered her with a patchwork quilt.

Dick remained out in the parlor, pacing back and forth like an expectant father. He implored Granny to send for an ambulance. She made him a calmative tea and ordered him to relax, which he did. He was so relaxed, in fact, that his own snores complimented the snorting of the pigs outside.

As the sun was setting and the heat of the day wore off, Lee emerged from Granny's bedroom, completely cool and returned to her own normal self. The swelling had all dissipated and the rash had totally disappeared. Lee felt as if she had been asleep for three days, totally refreshed. Even Dick was calm and not in the least tired.

"Okay, Granny," Dick said. "Fess up. What on earth did you give us in that tea? And, what was that weed juice that we put on Lee?"

Granny laughed. "Oh, Dick," she said, "Lee seems to have had a run in with some Poison Oak on your trek in here. What you put on her is "Jewel Weed," a remarkable wild plant that is a natural remedy for the poison. The tea was just a mixture of chamomile leaves, licorice bark and a few other herbs to calm you both down and bring down Lee's fever. It also helps with digestion when you have a big meal." Dick couldn't believe that Lee recovered so quickly-- and they didn't even have to visit or pay a hospital!

"However I do have one request," said Granny. "Please do me the pleasure of accepting my hospitality and staying the night, so I can be sure you are both okay for your return trip. I wouldn't want to lose any first-time patients!" Little did she know that this was the one wish that both Lee and Dick had secretly hoped Granny would request. But then again, they had heard stories of Granny also being a mind reader.

Needless to say, by the time Lee and Dick left (with photos of Granny, the dog, and even the pigs), they were both fairly knowledgeable in backwoods cures and remedies for a myriad of ills and aches. They promised to keep in touch, and to confirm all rumors of successful natural medicine practiced in the mountains.

Lee also learned to distinguish the difference between friendly green plants and her own private nemesis, poison oak. Dick took home a jar of crushed herbs for his calming tea, a balm that Granny Pickle assured, would make him live longer.

Chapter 10
New Orleans

New Orleans is the festive city of Mardi Gras, Cajun food, and a history rich in adventure. No less than twenty books filled an impressive space in Aunt Lee's library on this most lively part of the state of Louisiana. Once again, I settled into reading with my legs tucked underneath me, ready to inhale the aroma of colorful people and tight fisted tradition.

The next afternoon's session became one of the most exciting reenactments of Aunt Lee's adventures.

Lee was assigned to write an article about the famous celebration occurring every year just prior to Lent, Mardi Gras. An overbooked flight encouraged travelers to give up their tickets for free future flights and promises of amenities upon reaching their destination. Fellow passengers were all intended participants in the partying and revelry of Mardi Gras.

Frequent flights enabled my aunt to enjoy the privilege of first class seating for most of her adventures. This ensured confirmation of both her flight and her comfort.

The party atmosphere permeated each cabin as colorfully dressed flight attendants passed out spicy food and exotic drinks freely.

Just as the cabin doors began to close, it looked like Lee would have the peaceful trip that she desired. Instead, a frantic knocking caused the entire front cabin to turn to the center aisle. The door reopened and an animated vision wearing flame colored chiffon floated into first class. Billows of auburn curls floated over her shoulders and half way down her back. An expertly composed countenance turned to Lee and begged her pardon for the inconvenience. Lee charmingly acknowledged an impressive introduction.

The late passenger was Justine, the top costume designer at llaine Hartman's studio, the most famous costumery in New Orleans. Family hardship forced her to be absent for the most crucial week of her professional year, the week prior to Mardi Gras. She hurriedly performed last minute tasks on a fully loaded laptop while her rhinestone encrusted cellphone rang incessantly. Only when the captain announced the turning off of telephones during part of the flight, did Justine finally sit back in the comfortable leatherette seat. At this time, she formally introduced herself to my aunt and inquired about Lee's destination.

Lee gave her the brief introduction she reserved for acquaintances, but was soon enthralled with the charismatic personality she sat next to. As if they were old friends from a previous life, Lee and Justine quickly established a strong bond that delighted both of them. Cocktails and French cuisine relaxed the senses and kindled the beginning of a friendship that would surely endure.

By the end of the four hour flight, Justine had called and made reservations for Lee at the famed Bourbon Orleans Hotel on Bourbon Street. She kindly cancelled the confirmed reservations Lee had at a much more conservative hotel near the airport. At the flight's end Justine pecked each of Lee's cheeks and made her solemnly promise to spend time with her during her stay. Lee agreed.

Invitations to private parties for each night of Mardi Gras were forthcoming when Lee arrived at Bourbon Street. Festive activities were already underway as music and dancing ribboned through each alleyway and storefront.

Bougainvillea and magnolias hung lavishly both inside and outside of the hotel. Quaint gingerbread moldings and sparkling white paint adorned balustrades and banisters. Louis XV chairs with chintz seats and watered silk drapes adorned the lobby and sitting rooms. Overhead fans gently pushed the air around in an aromatic flurry of floral scents. Seated behind an ornate mahogany front desk was an ideal representative of Southern hospitality.

    Lee stated her name and signed the guest registry. Immediately a porter was dispatched to lead her to her suite and make sure she was comfortable. The suite was aptly named; three rooms decorated in exquisite French antiquity contained personal amenities that could please any guest. There was chilling wine, an over-filled fruit basket, and a tray with afternoon tea and tiny petit fours begging to be consumed. Vivaldi played softly as the ceiling fan slowly turned.

    However, the piece de resistance was certainly the bathroom. Daffodil yellow gauze curtains bordered in delicate lace covered the skylight. An old-fashioned claw footed tub was modernized with Jacuzzi jets. Warm yellow towels and a plush matching velour robe adorned the wooden dowels by the fireplace. Lemon soaps and bubbling bath crystals clustered in crystal containers on the marbleized dry sink. A hidden closet contained modern beauty tools like hair dryers, curling irons, and an electric razor. Lee was in heaven. She leisurely bathed and settled in the huge carved bed to eliminate her jet lag.

    Lee's schedueled wake up call jostled her from a very fitful rest. Minutes later the phone rang again. The concierge called to inform Lee that an invitation had been sent by messenger for a party that evening. The party was to be attended in costume, and one would be delivered to the hotel that afternoon.

    Lee was thrilled. Mardi Gras was exciting to attend, but to be invited to a private party was a boon to be appreciated.

    A light breakfast of buttery croissants and wafer thin cinnamon apple slices was enjoyed with syrupy thick coffee, laced with mocha.

    Thoroughly satisfied, Lee quickly dressed and checked her phone's email for messages. No surprises awaited her, so she left the hotel to check out some popular places of interest.

    The hotel was a mere block away from the Mississippi River. This fact prompted my aunt to walk toward that direction in the early morning coolness. Massive paddleboats, proudly held their slots at the docks. Workers scrubbed the colorful decks to erase any traces of river sludge and dew that might have sullied their appearance. Bells clanged and whistles blew, welcoming the day. The awakening sun beamed off the polished brass handrails. Commercial barges skimmed steadfastly through the water, carrying their heavy cargo. Lee imagined she could hear eerie spirituals and chants carried through the still air from the boats to the shore. A persistent foghorn woke her from the daydream.

Morning hours passed quickly and the sun rose in the sky to beam its vibrant rays on the earth. Quaint shops lining the riverside offered real and replicated versions of by-gone artifacts and curiosities. Hawkers with heads wrapped in colored silks offered fortunes and charms for good fortune and riches. While walking past a cheerfully-striped tent, Lee was summoned by the gold bedecked character who sat out front. Politeness encouraged Lee to step nearer to the tent. The woman, old and wrinkled like an un-ironed sheet, took Lee's hand and told her she was soon to meet a very handsome potential suitor. She warned Lee that her heart would not heed her head, and excitement leading to danger could occur. Lee laughed and tossed a few coins into the woman's battered tin cup.

A riverside outdoor cafe produced a cup of steaming bouillabaisse that warmed and spiced the senses. Cold tea with sprigs of fresh mint was served in a tall frosted glass.

The sun was high in the sky at this time and the streets were almost bare. Hats and sunglasses could not provide any relief from the baking rays of the sun. Lee agreed with the natives that an afternoon nap, in the shade, was the only way to cope with the elements this time of day. She retraced her steps back to the elegant hotel. The lobby was quiet, as everyone copied her intents. Leaving a request for a wake-up call, she entered the golden elevator.

Lee opened the door to her suite and saw that the beautiful lace coverlet had been turned back on the bed and a perfect tea rose was on her pillow. Two boudoir chairs held the promised costume, a lovely vision in periwinkle blue. The elegant gown was a perfect replica of one worn by the Empress Josephine. It was recognizable because Josephine had donned the original when she posed for a portrait with her lover, Napoleon. The high waistline and flowing silk fabric was laced with little seed pearls and satin forget-me-nots. The bosom was low and the sleeves puffy, but short. Long white gloves lay over the side of the chair. On the dressing table was a tawny brown wig, laden with ringlets and entwined with more seed pearls. A mask, exactly the same delicate shade of blue as the gown, sat on the table. A necklace and earrings, both complimentary shades of blue stones, were in two black velvet jewel boxes. A pillow on the carpet carried the most beautiful pair of silk evening slippers, again adorned with seed pearls. Hanging on the wardrobe was the most exquisite dark blue velvet hooded cape that Lee had ever seen.

An embossed envelope with the letter "J" lay on top of the jewel box holding the necklace. A similarly embossed sheet of magnolia scented paper beheld spidery script and read: "To my new found friend. Enjoy tonight and know that as soon as I set eyes on you, I was convinced that you had to wear this costume. If reincarnation is possible, then you have indeed come back to haunt us as the beautiful Empress Josephine. See you at the party."

Lee smiled and slid between the silk sheets of the canopied bed. Dreams of romance, pirates, and parties laced through her fitful nap. Only once did she not smile in her sleep when, during a slow waltz, a small wrinkled old woman ran up to her and said, "Remember, beware!" Lee turned over and quickly fell back into a peaceful sleep.

Bells tinkled and Lee suddenly realized that the telephone was ringing. It was the front desk, fulfilling her request to be awoken at 4 pm. A leisurely bath in water sprinkled with jasmine bath beads relaxed her. She then enveloped herself in the velour robe and towel dried her hair. Welcoming the delivery of high tea, Lee sat out on the balcony where delicate pâté and wafers were served with juicy strawberries and cream. Cafe au lait ended the repast, and Lee was ready to begin preparations for the soiree.

The entire outfit complimented Lee's skin tone and enhanced the vision of total femininity. Even the curls of the wig encircled her face with soft beauty. Lee couldn't stop looking in the mirror at her reflection. At 8 pm the front desk announced her limousine, and Lee was on her way to the ball, just like Cinderella.

The festivties were to be held in the ballroom of an old plantation, restored and refurbished with period furniture. Limosines, town cars, classic cars and sports cars drove up to the portico, discharged their guests, and were driven off to unseen parking places. Unescorted ladies were walked up the stairs and accompanied until they were announced. A beautiful center staircase, banisters entwined with garlands of wildflowers, spilled out on to a mirror shined parquet floor. Figures dressed as kings, queens, mimes and feathered peacocks whirled around the floor as an orchestra of Washingtonian musicians graced the stage. Ice sculptures and flower creations graced tabletops on either side of the rotunda shaped room. Sparkling crystal chandeliers shared space with nets of balloons and streamers, to be released at a later time. Wigged waiters and waitresses stood at every doorway to dispatch champagne and caviar.

Lee was mesmerized by the whole spectacle. Within seconds a costumed cavalier, handsomely dressed as a gentleman pirate sporting a black satin mask, asked her to dance. She nodded ascent and was quickly whisked out to the center of the floor. While whirling around, Lee could not take her eyes off her partner. He was very tall, muscular but lean, and performed the old fashioned waltz steps with smooth expertise. His face, not entirely hidden by the mask, was tanned and a well-trimmed mustache bordered finely sculptured lips. Deep grooves pierced his cheeks as he smiled and a finely chiseled nose boasted aristocratic heritage. Undoubtedly, Lee and her partner captured the ambiance of the night and were envied by all who were there. The dance was swiftly followed by another and then another, and the night ambled on without either partner tiring or wanting the fun to end. But at the end of a particularly rousing polka, a gong was heard and dinner was announced.

All couples herded towards a beautiful sunroom that had been transformed into a dining room. Tables of varied sizes lined two of the glass walls. A tremendous buffet of glazed ham, smoked turkey, salmon and filets of beef were surrounded by platters of grilled vegetables and fresh fruit. Punch flowed from cherub fountains and cream pastries held up the rear. Thick black coffee, so hot it had to be sipped cautiously filled silver urns.

Lee and her mystery man filled their plates and found a small table for two beside a tall column. Having danced for hours, they needed food and drink to replenish their energy. Food was consumed with gusto while minimal small talk was made throughout endless courses. Lee's curiosity piqued more and more as her new friend kept his mask on throughout the meal. He was thoroughly entranced when she removed hers, but steadfastly refused to do likewise.

Pleasantly full, the striking couple decided to simultaneously stretch their legs. Gardens of lilies and fragrant gardenias lined walkways of cobblestones. The couple gently touched fingers as the path led to a beautiful gazebo, away from the festivities. Privacy was achieved as the gazebo was surrounded by huge, swaying weeping willows, swinging their long limbs in the cool breeze. Whitewashed benches filled the surrounding lattices. The couple sat in silence, neither wanting the night to end.

Natural curiosity caused Lee to break the silence. Just as she was about to ask her mysterious, handsome man who he was, the band struck up a sensuous Tango. He laughed, leaned over and whispered in her ear, "Just call me Jean LaFitte, my petite fille." The buccaneer then immediately encircled her waist with one muscular arm and whirled her off to the dance floor. Once again his graceful form encouraged her body to flow with unleashed rhythm. Talk was impossible. Uninhibited enjoyment caused her cheeks to flush and her skin to overheat.

The Latin set of dances began with a Tango, followed by a sultry Salsa and ended with a Cha Cha. Soon everyone got up to dance the Conga, in which they held onto each others' waists and formed an enormous snake line. The undulating line of dancers wove in and out of tables, chairs, and even the orchestra's stage. Waiters, musicians, even the coat check staff joined in the celebration.

The exhausting dance ended and everyone's goodbyes could be overheard throughout the crowd; people hugged and kissed and reluctantly headed to the stairway to begin their ascents to the portico and await their rides.

Lee blotted the beads of perspiration from her brow and pushed back the damp ringlets of her fancy hairpiece. Seeing a nearby restroom, she quickly ran inside to repair her disheveled appearance.

Cooler and calmer, Lee left the ladies lounge and looked around the ballroom for her enigmatic dance partner. To her dismay, he was nowhere to be found. She searched each room and even behind the stage.

More than slightly embarrassed, Lee ascended the stairs towards the massive portico. Her limosine arrived immediately and she entered the gleaming silver vehicle. At the hotel, the driver ran around to the door and opened it for Lee, as the doorman performed the same action. As she headed for the golden elevators once more, a voice called out, "Excuse me, mademoiselle!" Lee turned around towards the front desk and the bellman handed her a perfect long stemmed red rose with an attached note. The note read: [1] *'To my beautiful Josephine, Thank you for the most enchanting evening. May we meet again, someday. Ever adoring you, Captain Jean LaFitte."*

Lee never did find out who her elusive party partner was. However, a trip to the local library produced a portrait of the famous pirate, Jean LaFitte. She gasped at the uncanny likeness to her handsome dancing buccaneer. No one in New Orleans would claim to know of his whereabouts or even of his existence.

Lee wonders to this day.

Chapter 11
Africa

Aunt Lee felt a beckoning from deep within the pulsating heart of the dark continent of Africa. She had been summoned by her editor to plan a rudimentary trip there for the purpose of enticing travelers to this remote area of the world. Tourism rates had steadily declined in this region of lush rainforests, thus travel experts were consulted, and agreements and contracts were offered to lure vacationers and students with attractive travel packages.

Lee's destination was the Pare National des Volcans in Rwanda, the home of the Virunga mountain chain and the mountain gorilla. Her excitement was great, as she had followed the life story of Dian Fossey from the beginning to its tragic end. Dian's former home, the Karisoke Research Center, had been the epicenter of many years of intense study on these magnificent primates. The book "Gorillas in the Mist" glamorized and revealed the mystique of this ancient land and the gentle intelligence of the species living there.

Lee chose many articles and press releases to read on the long journey to this tropical land. She researched everything about her new subjects, including their habitats, eating preferences, social interactions, and their all-too-common death due to the terrible act of poaching.

Lee became so involved that she hardly noticed the hours slipping away; a sudden announcement jolted her from immersion into primate life and back to the reality of arriving at their destination. Lee quickly stuffed her research papers into her briefcase and prepared to explore a fascinating country.

The first obstacle that greeted Lee was the oppressive heat. Although forewarned of what temperatures to expect, the sudden pelting of arid air caused her to gulp for air. She knew it would take a few days for her body to adjust to the change from New York's urban air to this tropical, humid stillness. Walking slowly and deliberately taking shorter breaths helped her adapt to the change. This was further complicated because while holding two travel bags and a briefcase, Lee joined her fellow travelers in swatting swarms of dive-bombing black flies. She had wisely refrained from using any perfumes or scented cosmetics, as the onslaught of flying insects were more attracted to others in the group who had not been warned of such an attack. However, a steady stream of pesky invaders still dove around her head.

Soldiers both on foot and in jeeps surrounded the perimeter of the airport, evidence of civil war was everywhere Lee looked. Poverty and starvation were vividly exposed at the marketplace beside the landing strip; orphans and the elderly openly begged for food and clothing next to stalls of vibrant colored cloth and newly picked vegetables. Sad faces implored others for help and stick-like arms reached out for alms. Lee's spirits were quickly falling.

While struggling along with throngs of people, Lee abruptly encountered a tall, ebony-skinned man in khaki colored shorts and a bush hat. He saluted her and announced, in English, "Welcome Mademoiselle, I am Toshimbe, your guide." He continued, "Please follow me to your jeep," as he gently relieved her of her baggage. Lee smiled with relief and felt a surge of energy as she followed the well-mannered man on their quest. However she soon discovered that Toshimbe had practiced these two sentences for weeks; his native language was Swahili and in order to qualify for this job he had to be able to speak in English. Lee had invested in a "Learn Swahili" tape and had been practicing the speech inflections for a month. What fun they both had trying to understand each other for the next three weeks! Fortunately Lee was both a talented teacher and student, as was Toshimbe. Sign language and gestures proved effective communicators many times throughout their expedition.

Weaving and bobbing through the hoards of people, Lee and Toshimbe finally reached the jeep. It was very similar to the vintage army jeeps Lee had seen in old war movies. The canvas top consisted of more holes than canvas. Toshimbe laughed while pointing to the largest hole and said, "Air conditioning, Mademoiselle." Lee rolled her eyes and laughed too. He quickly put Lee's luggage into the back seat and tied ropes around them. Lee would soon find out why this extra measure of safety was necessary.

Toshimbe held Lee's arm as she climbed over the front passenger's door, as it was rusted shut and this was the only way to get in. He then ran quickly around to the driver's side and nimbly jumped into his seat (over the other rusted shut door).

With a shout of "We go!" Toshimbe popped the clutch and bucked the little vehicle into rapid movement. The sounds of planes landing and loud people prevented Lee from asking any questions until they were well out of range of the airport. Several miles later the road became quite desolate and Lee was able garner his attention. "Toshimbe," she hollered, "how long do we have to ride on this road until we begin the ascent to the mountains?" "Not long, Mademoiselle," he said, "only about four more hours!" Lee groaned as the well-rutted roads went on and on. They passed migrating people with all of their belongings in baskets on their heads, and although they knew their fates were uncertain, they ambled along singing with smiles on their faces. Children gathered sticks and tossed stones into the dense vegetation on the sides of the road. When asked, Toshimbe said that these were homeless people who had been uprooted by the civil war. Too sad to imagine the consequences, Lee resisted asking any more questions.

More than four hours later, Toshimbe veered sharply left onto a one-lane road, almost causing Lee to lose her straw hat. The jeep felt like it was about to flip, once Toshimbe regained control of the vehicle he slowed down considerably. He then explained, 'We are now at the base of the mountain, Mademoiselle. Soon you will see a place where we can stop for the night." All Lee could think of, with horror, were half-burned-out thatched huts with outdoor plumbing.

Roughly one mile later Lee was pleasantly surprised by the appearance of a lovely old plantation home. There were wonderful gardens and a tropical topiary surrounding the premises. The house was pale yellow and a white-screened gazebo stood off to one side, with occupants enjoying afternoon tea. Yellow and white striped canopies were draped over the verandah surrounding the huge home. White painted rocking chairs and bamboo tables completed a picture of tropical splendor.

Embarrassed by her disheveled appearance, Lee reached for her comb and lipstick, while brushing the road dust off from her clothes. A cursory look in a pocket mirror revealed that her efforts were futile. She threw up her hands and abandoned the quest.

Just then Lee heard a happy voice shout, "Ah, Miss Farthingale, I presume?" Lee nodded and said, "Yes, I am Lee Farthingale." "My name is Leakey," the gentleman stated, to Lee's shock. "No, no," he laughed, "not THE Leakey you are thinking of. I am Thomas Leakey, proprietor of this homestead, and absolutely no relation to Dr. or Mrs. Leakey, of international fame. I have introduced myself in exactly this way for over ten years, and still enjoy the shock on my guest's faces! That being said, I hope you enjoy your stay here in my home, and please feel free to advise me if any of your needs are not met."

After a good laugh, Lee was shown to her room on the second floor of the house. In fact, it could be considered a suite of rooms. The large bedroom, complete with canopied bed, was complimented by a sitting room and private bath. Off to the side of the sitting room was a screened balcony, which beheld two bamboo rockers and a lovely white cane table. The view of the Virunga mountains was spectacular. The mist which surrounded the mountains was not at its thickest yet, so she enjoyed the views of steep slopes and dense vegetation all around her. Her excitement mounted as she heard distant animal sounds and musical bird songs. Was it her imagination, or did she hear drums too?

A quick shower and light supper later, Lee and Toshimbe joined their host on the verandah for iced coffee. The air was cooler and the sounds of the mountains surrounding them were soothing. Mr. Leakey offered tales and anecdotes of the years when Dian Fossey lived on the mountain with her beloved gorillas. He gave Lee suggestions for tours and was willing to include his beautiful homestead as part of the incentive for prospective travelers. She considered his advice valuable and soon graciously excused herself to write some notes and catch up on sleep. Tomorrow would be another full day.

To avoid the midday sun, Lee agreed with Toshimbe to start up the mountain very early in the morning. Most visitors wisely did the same, so early breakfast was always available. In fact, boxed lunches were provided also, as most of the visitors would plan to be out in the wilderness for the majority of the day.

Laden with the food, insect repellent, cameras, and binoculars, Lee and her guide topped off the gas tank of the jeep and started on their journey. Stout water-proofed boots and rain parkas were standard wardrobe for everyone attempting to conquer the slopes. Layers of clothing that could be systematically removed as the temperature rose was considered the uniform of the day. The magazine had provided Lee with the funds for a pre-trip shopping spree where she gladly indulged in appropriate gear for the trek. The last necessary item kept close at hand was Lee's tiny hand held tape recorder. She knew that this was the best way to keep notes in remote places, it was so sensitive that Lee could whisper in a very low voice and still create a reliable recording.

Waving goodbye to Mr. Leakey, they once more checked their maps, and began the journey upwards. Luckily Mr. Leakey was kind enough to point out recognizable landmarks on the map. The vegetation was always so thick and constantly growing that many times the narrow road was almost entirely covered over. But Toshimbe's experience and Mr. Leakey's advice would prove to remove them from any potentially dangerous situation.

Up the mountain the straining jeep crawled. Now and then Toshimbe would put the vehicle in park and jump out to clear the roadway of debris that had fallen during the last rainfall. This made for very slow progress. Lee didn't mind the interruptions though, because she wanted to drink in the local flavor of all the beautiful wild flowers surrounding the trail. Glimpses of small wildlife also peeked out from underneath mossy hiding places and from behind berry bushes. Monkeys with manlike faces swung from vines or ran up mile high trees.

With binoculars she caught sight of a pair of bushbuck antelopes resting in a clearing, their ears raised in cautious attention. These graceful animals were all too often the victims of greedy poachers who left crippling snares all over the forest. However Dian Fossey's tireless work has helped save a goodly number of these beautiful creatures from extinction.

As they rose higher and higher up the mountain the air grew thinner and moister. Lee and Toshimbe shed their jackets, but kept their shirts' sleeves rolled down and buttoned as barriers against insects and nettles. Even inside the jeep, low hanging vegetation crept through the holes in the canvas top. At one point Lee gasped and Toshimbe reached up to grab a small, colorful snake that had fallen off a branch and landed on top of Lee's straw hat. He expertly flicked the unwanted guest away, and back into the habitat where it belonged. Once her heartbeat slowed down, Lee breathed a sigh of relief. Toshimbe just smiled a toothy grin and wisely kept quiet.

When the sun seemed to be at its hottest, they conveniently reached their final destination, the Karisoke Research Center. Luckily, they were expecting Lee. A special guided tour of the center afforded her the opportunity to pay her respects to the graves of Dian Fossey and her beloved gorilla Digit. Lee remembered Dian's book and the wonderful diaries she kept on the magnificent creature and her magical relationship with him. In Lee's eyes, no one could ever match the accomplishments Dian conquered with the animal species. Had he known and observed her research, Darwin would most certainly have had much more material to prove his theories about early civilization.

The research center had changed remarkably since Dian's death. Tourist interaction was now encouraged, mainly for financial support. The once reclusive station was now renovated to accept tours with trained guides. Daily hikes deep into gorilla country were scheduled. Lee and Toshimbe joined a pre arranged tour with seven other people to see first hand the gentle giants in their natural habitat. Warnings were issued prior to the tour and releases were signed. Weapons were forbidden, although the guide did have a tranquilizer gun for emergency use. He was careful and proud to say that he had never, in all his five years as a guide, used the gun. The tourists were given instructions about any possible interaction that might occur between themselves and the animals. This lecture lasted one full hour and an additional half-hour was scheduled for questions and answers. Full precautions were taken.

A final clothing and footgear inspection of the tourists ended the indoctrination and the trek began. The guide led the group and at times hacked out overgrown brush from the trails. He pointed out the giant lobelia trees, whose leaves were favorites to the gorillas out of which to build sleeping nests. The trees were massive and the leaves thick as leather. Hagenia trees, ancient and massive, sometimes held openings at their bases that looked like caves. The guide said that poachers would hide in these trees and await unsuspecting animals to be caught in their snares.

Gorillas spend their days eating, sleeping, and traveling to find other food sources, thus they can be tracked to the areas where the tastiest food grows. Deeper into the forest we came upon some discarded sleep nests and piles of gorilla dung, not too old to have lost its pungent aroma. Excitement rose among the group. A reminder of the need for quiet was rewarded a short time later when the guide motioned for everyone to remain still. Hunched down and surreptitiously attentive, everyone stared into the thick underbrush with awe and disbelief. Not thirty feet away was a small group of gorillas, black as the night, eating succulent bamboo shoots. They patiently stripped the shoots of their stringy stalks and enjoyed every last drop of the pulpy insides. Youngsters imitated their elders and then enjoyed the feast. Infants hung on to their mothers' bellies, while nursing and watching their moms eat. Only sounds of ardent chewing and an occasional belch could be heard as the troop replenished its nourishment. So docile did the group appear, that one of the members of the tour group forgot his instructions and suddenly rose up to shake out a cramped leg.

Within seconds of his action, off to the left of the group of primates a large bush began to rattle and a tremendous roar emerged! Suddenly from out of the foliage a huge 300-pound silver back came charging directly towards the tour group! He alternately screamed and beat his chest as he ran on all fours! "Poc, poc, poc," his chest beat sounded like a machine gun barking. The group panicked and ran for the trees, exactly the opposite of what they had been instructed to do. Only Lee and Toshimbe froze in their tracks, kept their eyes downward, and hunched down in a submissive posture. Not five feet in front of them the massive beast halted and just stared at the intruders, he was so close they could smell him. Lee peeked sideways at him and watched as he stared, sniffed, and grunted. To their surprise, the giant ambled closer on his forearms, reached out a leathery palm, and poked Lee's hand. On the inside Lee shivered, but she held her ground firmly and remained composed. A few sniffs later the simian leader turned around and slowly retreated. However, after roughly ten steps, he rapidly turned around, stood up, and beat his chest one more time, as if to say, "This is my home and you will respect me!" He turned and walked away into the forest behind his group.

Lee waited until the silver back was totally out of sight before she moved, and then she slowly collapsed onto a nearby rockbed. Totally drenched in sweat, she regained her composure and reflected on the remarkable events that had just transpired. By then Toshimbe was at her side with a canteen of water and a soaked cloth, ready to calm her, but Lee just needed to be still and meditate on the beauty and power of these creatures. "Wild and uncivilized?" she thought. "Oh, no! Not these species," she decided, "humans have a lot to learn from them about socialization and respect for others." From that moment she promised herself to further study these wonderful creatures and help their plight in whatever way she could.

The group was thoroughly satisfied with their tour and quite ready to return to the research center, most were even ready to cut their vacations short and schedule returns all the way back to the plantation. However, Lee and Toshimbe stayed at the research center for several more days and hoped to see more of the gentle apes. A few more sightings occured, but nothing like the first day of the tour. However, Lee was satisfied with her discoveries and was anxious to write about the events. Fortunately, she had flicked on her recording device just before her encounter with the silver back, providing her with vivid proof of the experience.

Upon her arrival at the Plantation house, Lee was greeted with shouts of congratulations. The tale of her encounter with the silver back had filtered down the mountain and become common knowledge throughout the town. Natives were starting to wonder if there was a connection between dark haired women and the gorillas; not since Dian Fossey had they heard of anyone having such a close meeting with a silver back and surviving to tell of it. The news had even traveled across the globe, as a telegram from her editor arrived the next day. Lee was a celebrity amongst the National Geographic crowd, but to Lee, the notoriety came second to the pride she felt having had her very own personal interaction with a real mountain gorilla.

Chapter 12
Conclusion

One balmy spring afternoon, Aunt Lee's editor, Ed, appeared at the townhouse. We were about half way through tea when Matthew announced his presence. Lee was having a lucid day, so she was flirtatious and giddy when she saw her old boss. She asked him to join us, and sent Matthew downstairs for another china place setting.

Ed promptly enjoyed two slices of the spongy yellow tea bread and waved away the sugar bowl when offered for his tea. "Strong and bitter is how I like it," he said. "I like to savor the real flavor of my tea," he continued, "earl grey has a perfume, exotic taste that needs to be appreciated without additives.

At least that is how I like it!" Lee nodded in appreciation, but continued to lightly sweeten her cup. I too followed suit.

After paying homage to their afternoon ritual, the satiated man rose, and with hands in his pockets paced throughout the room while voicing the reason for his visit. He was not known to indulge in social visits, so both Lee and Cassie knew something was up.

"My friends," he said, "I come here both in friendship and with a business proposition. Lee, I have been watching your niece grow under your tutelage and guidance this past year." He continued, "After reading several drafts of your journal, I have met with the chairman

CONCLUSION

and trustees of our magazine. We feel that the legacy you are passing on to Cassie must not go on without recognition and support. Therefore, we have decided to offer you both a deal which will benefit everyone!"

"Lee," he said, "your readers are anxious to continue hearing from you on a regular basis. So we would like you to consider writing a small article in every edition of the magazine which will keep your faithful followers happy. The contents of the article will chronicle the progress of Cassie, who will be your successor in the travel business."

He smiled and continued, "Cassie, your talent is evident and the magazine would like to be your mentor and sponsor you with a full scholarship to the college of your choice, pursuing studies in foreign cultures and journalism. You will continue your Aunt's legacy, and add new adventures of your own once you feel comfortable ." He pleaded, "I hope that you will continue to be part of this great global literary family, and be willing to share your experiences with as many people as possible. I'll leave you now to think about it, hopefully you will accept my offer." Matthew accompanied Ed downstairs and to his car. I stood at the upstairs window and waved heartily.

Both Aunt Lee and I could hardly contain our joy! I imagined a future beyond my wildest dreams, and Aunt Lee was was able to gracefully accept whatever life had in store for the both of us.

I hugged Aunt Lee and excused myself to go write a long letter to Josh, telling him about the exciting proposition that has just taken place. However, Aunt Lee held me back. "Cassie," she implored, "I think one more little amendment should be added to our agreement with the magazine." I couldn't think of anything that Ed had left out of the package. Puzzled, I sat down on the edge of Aunt Lee's lounge and listened.

"As we are both now to be big time travel writers, I think we are going to need a manager to handle arrangements for us," she said. "We will need a level-headed person to keep our appointments straight, our financial accounts balanced, and chiefly to ensure that our lives retain some kind of normalcy. I know how easy it is to get caught up in travel and writing about it, so much so that you forget important things like family, holidays, and simply to enjoy your own life. So perhaps we need another person to keep things in order. What do you think?"

I admitted that I hadn't given a single thought to this part of our lives, I naively just assumed that Aunt Lee knew how to handle it all, without any help. After contemplating this I replied, "Yes, you are so right as usual, Aunt Lee! But who could do all of this and want to work exclusively with us?"

Lee smiled and said, "How about your brother Josh? He is about to finish his schooling and is quite proficient in accounting and management. I'm sure we could trust him with our lives." I reached over and hugged my Aunt while shouting, "Yes, yes, that is the perfect decision! Thank you! Now I must go write Josh and tell him the news!"

Lee sank back onto her pillows, reaching underneath one to retrieve something. She withdrew a wrinkled envelope containing a single page.

Rereading the page once more, she smiled and thought to herself, "Well, my dear sister, I'm keeping my part of our bargain. I promised you many years ago to be a guardian angel to your two children, and finally I am able to keep my vow. Hopefully, I will be around for a while longer to make sure they are protected and well on their way in this big world. You can rest easy now knowing that I will shelter them the best that I can, and provide guidance when it is needed." She tucked the sheet back into the envelope and placed it back under the pillow. Peacefully, sleep took over her mind.

About the Author

As a young girl growing up in New Jersey, Marie Therese was an avid reader using books as an escape, dreaming of someday writing works of her own.

First inspired to write by Louisa May Alcott, after reading *Little Women*, Marie finally put pen to paper when an opportunity to merge her two passions presented itself. As a collector of Vintage Costume Jewelry and an Instructor of Jewelry Creation and Design, she began her career as an author by writing articles for Vintage Fashion Costume Jewelry magazine once the magazine's editor, Lucille Tempesta, encouraged her. Through the support of her friends and family, especially her daughter Kristen who told her to "never give up", Marie Therese realized her dream of writing *The Mysterious Letter: Aunt Lee's Legacy*, her first novel.

Marie Therese's writing encourages her readers to embrace both the faith and hope that life's obstacles and crisis' can be overcome with one simple turn of events.